THIS SONG IS (NOT) FOR YOU

LAURA NOWLIN

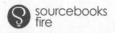

sourcebooks
fire

Published by Sourcebooks Fire, an imprint of Sourcebooks, Inc.
P.O. Box 4410, Naperville, Illinois 60567-4410
(630) 961-3900
Fax: (630) 961-2168
www.sourcebooks.com

The Library of Congress Cataloging-in-Publication data is on file with the publisher.

Printed and bound in the United States of America.

VP 10 9 8 7 6 5 4 3 2 1

This book is (totally) for

the Icebergs,

the kick-ass, avant-garde, in-your-face

experimental noise rock band

that let me hang out during practice

and call it "research for my novel."

Robert Rosener,

Ausin Case,

and

Brad Schumacher, a.k.a. the Night Grinder.

Thanks, guys.

(But if you've read this book before

and you're reading it again,

then this time,

the song is for you.)

♡xoRamona

Have you ever met someone and you could feel that they were going to be important to you? It's like you never knew it, but you've been waiting your whole life to meet this person, and you recognize him with the same ease that you recognize your reflection.

That happened to me once.

When Sam told me his name, I laughed. It was like I should have already known. It was like he was already my Sam.

"Sorry," I said. "I'm not laughing at you."

"What are you laughing at?" he asked. We were standing on the stairwell outside the music department. Some guy knocked into his shoulder, but Sam didn't react. When Sam is interested in something, it's like the whole rest of the world has ceased to exist.

"It's just, I feel like I should have already known that. You look like a Sam. Does that make sense?" I asked.

"No," Sam said, and he gave me my first crooked smile. We were both freshmen, and it was the first day of school.

"I'm Ramona," I said.

"That makes sense," he said.

"I said that?" Sam asks. He frowns at his guitar. He's replacing the B string, so I only have about one-eighth of his attention right now.

"Yeah, it was like we already knew each other's names or something." And then quieter, 'cause I'm not sure if I want him to hear or not, "Or felt each other's names."

Sam continues to frown at his guitar. I drum an impatient six-eighths beat on the garage floor. "Hurry up," I say. "Nanami is waiting for us."

Nanami is our band's biggest and only fan. Whenever we post a new video on our web page, she comments immediately the next day. Someday when April and the Rain is super famous, we're going to go to Japan on tour and meet her in person—and she will be thrilled.

Anyway.

I move my drumming off the floor and onto Sam's sneaker. He doesn't react.

"So, are we skipping band practice tomorrow?" I ask.

"Why would we?" He finally looks up at me, and when I see his eyes, I feel the familiar flutter in my chest. Sam has brown, sleepy eyes fringed with long, black lashes.

"'Cause we're going to Artibus tomorrow! Did you forget?"

"No," Sam says. "But I don't see why we should skip practice. If anything, it should make us want to practice more."

For years Sam and I have dreamed of escaping Saint Joseph's Prep for the campus of Artibus College of Music and Arts. In case you don't know, high school sucks. Our high school especially, because it's full of rich kids—and the only thing worse than a poseur is a poseur with money. Sam and I don't hang out much with anybody else.

We're finally about to start our senior year. Summer is almost over, but first we have the admission evaluation tomorrow. School will start, and before we know it, we'll be applying for admission over winter break. The end is in sight.

"Almost done," he says.

I speed up my drumming on his foot.

"Ow! Okay, I'm done! Jeez, woman."

"You know you love me," I say.

"Yeah, yeah," he says, but he gives me that crooked smile, and I know it's true. I just wish it were a different sort of love.

It only took two days of being friends with Sam for us to start our band. In a month, he was the best friend I'd ever had. After a month and a half, I knew I was crushing on him hard, but I figured I'd get over it. I wasn't going to put the band at risk just because I was having girlie feelings.

By the time April and the Rain was a year old, I had to admit that I was in love with Sam. We were sophomores, we'd put up our website, and we'd told our asinine class-mates a hundred times that no, we weren't dating.

Up in Sam's room, we post this week's video. Yesterday Sam came up with a killer riff, and today we played it in a bunch of different tempos, so I got to do some pretty cool tricks on my kit. Nanami is gonna love it.

"We need to keep practicing this one," Sam says. "I wish we had just one more person to fill it out, maybe do a little vocal work." Sam is always saying this, but I don't think that lightning will strike us again. We were lucky enough to find each other.

Sam

Ramona was sleeping twenty-five minutes into the trip. I knew she would fall asleep. She always does when she has to be in a car for more than twenty minutes, and Artibus is an hour outside St. Louis.

Her mouth was hanging open, and she was frowning like she was dreaming of something that pisses her off, like dubstep.

She looked cute, but as a rule I try to ignore that. I turned up the radio.

"No," she groaned.

"We're almost there," I said. "You're gonna make a great impression at Artibus with dried-up drool on your face." Ramona wiped her mouth with the back of her hand and sat up in her seat.

"How close are we?"

"We're at the edge of town now. We have time to eat."

"Cool. Let's find a greasy diner that can be our place next year. We'll go there so much that all the waitresses will know our names."

I laughed. It was such a Ramona thing to say.

"Okay," I said. "Let me know when you see this place."

And before long, we did come by an appropriate-looking diner. The building was low to the ground and tucked back from the road. There was a semi in the parking lot and some half-wilted flowers in a pot by the door. The apostrophe and letter *S* on the neon sign had burned out.

"There!" Ramona pointed out the window. "Wanda Diner."

"Wanda's Diner."

"That's not what the sign says!"

I rolled my eyes and pulled into the parking lot.

It's always like that with Ramona. She gets an idea, and then it happens. Like with April and the Rain. This one afternoon early freshman year, we were outside Saint Joe's watching all the cars pull away, and she just announced, "We're gonna start a band."

"What?" I said. I was still baffled about why this pretty girl was hanging out with me. We only had one class together, but she always seemed to find me in the hallways, and that day in the lunchroom, she'd plopped down in the seat next to mine and started explaining riot grrrl's influence on Nirvana. Later in the lunch hour, I'd learned that she was at Saint Joe's as a faculty brat. Her dad taught Honors English and her mom was dead. But she said a lot less about both of them than she did about Kurt Cobain.

"A band," Ramona said. "You and me. You'll lead with whatever guitar you want. I'll play the drums. I'm really good."

"Maybe I'm not that good," I said. "What about that?"

"You're gonna be great," she said. "We should get started tonight. I can come over, right?"

"Hello, Janet," Ramona said to the waitress at our table. Janet glanced down at her name tag and looked at us skeptically over her notepad. "So, what's good today?"

"Chili's okay," Janet said. "But it's okay every day."

"I'm Ramona," Ramona said. "And this is my friend Sam. You're going to be seeing a lot of us."

"I think we need a minute," I said.

Janet shrugged and walked away.

"Well, I think she'll remember you," I said. "As a lunatic."

"It's a start," Ramona said. She smiled at me, and I had to look down at the menu.

Tom

Artibus looks okay. It's trying a little too hard to be a picturesque private college. The grass and trees have that traumatized look of too much fertilizer and regular trimming, and the sidewalks are disturbingly white.

I arrived early and have been sitting in my car for twenty minutes now. It's too humid to be outside for any length of time. I'm listening to Autechre, which helps.

Sara hated Autechre. "This song is creepy," she would say. "This is Autechre, isn't it?"

But now I'm remembering how much Sara hated Autechre, so I push the Skip button. Nils Petter Molvaer. Sara detested Molvaer.

Sara liked some good music, like Animal Collective. She also liked some really bad music, but most people do. And she liked that I was a musician. She was sweet and passionate about changing the world. That's what I liked best about her.

But that still is what I like best about her. She's not dead. She just broke up with me. She's still out there liking her good and bad music and not understanding the difference, probably changing the song if something I gave her comes up on random.

Some guy on the sidewalk makes a weird face at my car. He doesn't like Molvaer either. Or maybe it's just my car. My car is part of a long-term art project that I call "Glitter in Odd Places," or "GOP" for short. The objective is to influence society's perception of glitter by introducing glitter enhancements to customarily nonsparkly items or situations. I used to take Sara out with me glitter bombing.

I pull the keys out of the ignition.

The music department is easy to find; it's the biggest building on campus. It's so hot outside that opening the front door feels like opening a refrigerator and stepping inside. There's a sign right in front, "Admission Evaluations," and a little arrow pointing to the left. Apparently, someone was worried that we would all get lost and wander around bothering the real students, because I don't have to walk very far before coming to another sign pointing me in the direction I was already walking. A third sign leads me down a flight of stairs. "Basement," the worried person has added in ballpoint pen.

There's a small enclave with folding chairs. A woman who must be a parent is reading a book by the door. A guy and a girl my age are sitting in the corner whispering to each other. The guy has a guitar case, but the girl doesn't have an instrument. She's probably his enthusiastic and supportive girlfriend. I slump down in a chair far away from everyone else and close my eyes.

I open my eyes when I hear the door open. A girl comes out carrying a violin case and biting her lip. The woman stands and puts her arm around the girl. They whisper together as they walk up the stairs.

"Ramona Andrews?" A man with a clipboard is standing at the door now. The girl jumps up like she's been waiting her whole life for this man to come for her. They disappear into the room together. The guy and I are alone now, but he's bent over studying his shoelaces like they hold the secret to everything, so I doubt he's going to be a bother. I lean my head back against the wall and close my eyes again.

❧

The thing about Sara is that at first I didn't think I would like her at all. She's kinda cheerful, and usually I don't like cheerful people because they aren't really cheerful—they're just fake. But Sara really was just like that. *Is* just like that.

We met, of all the stupid places people can meet, at a shopping center. I'd made the mistake of thinking that my sneakers were my own property to do with as I wished. I'd written the word "Darfur" over and over again on my left shoe and "Auschwitz" all over the right shoe. Then I'd designed and printed fifty copies of my own four-by-four informative pamphlet entitled "Darfur and Other Holocausts You Might Not Know About!" to hand out to anyone who asked about my shoes. It was my first PSA (public service art) and I was very enthused.

My mother had sworn with tears in her eyes that I needed to buy new shoes tomorrow (*tomorrow*) or she would lose her faith in all that was good. (Though further discussion had resulted in an agreement that I could wear my PSA shoes and go out in public in my own free time, but no, not at school.) That was on a Friday night. On Saturday morning (yeah, morning) I drove to the mall. And I promised myself that I would buy the first pair of shoes that I didn't hate.

So I was staring at this wall of shoes, and this girl with a smile and a name tag came up to me.

"Can I help you?" she asked. And she was pretty (*is* pretty), but I've known a lot of pretty girls—or at least enough to be suspicious. I said that I kind of liked these one shoes but not really, and her face lit up. She said, "We have them in a darker color!"

And I could tell that she really was pleased. So I said okay, and she rushed off like she was on a mission. When she came back, I was surprised that I felt weird about taking my shoes off in front of her. I put the shoes on, and yeah, I didn't hate them.

"Okay," I said.

"Really?" She was so excited, and it really was sincere. She was like that even while ringing me up. I remember thinking that I'd never encountered somebody who could be that genuine with a stranger.

(I can be a bit prejudiced against people. I realized that about myself after being with Sara for a while.)

"By the way," she said, "I like your old shoes. A lot of people don't know about Darfur, or even what happened in Bosnia."

I hear the door open. The girl comes into the hall. The shoelace-staring guy stands up. She grins at him and they high-five. The one professor dude from before says, "Samuel Peterson," and then they high-five again. It is so fucking dorky that it has to be a real awesome moment for them. The guy and the professor walk into the room. When the door closes, the girl turns to me as if it is inevitable that we must speak.

"Hey," she says. "I like what you did to your sneakers."

"Thanks," I say. "I have a pamphlet."

She gets up and sits down a seat away from me. I hand the pamphlet to her and she studies it for a moment.

"I'm probably totally not adequately informed about global genocides," she says. "I'm definitely going to read this." Then she stretches her legs out in front of her and wiggles her toes inside her sandals. Her toenail polish is a chipped rainbow. "I'm auditioning for piano," she says.

"I'm being evaluated for a general music major," I hear myself saying. "They don't have a program for what I really do."

"Really? How are they going evaluate you? Are you nervous? What *do* you *do*? I play drums!"

This girl needs pixie ears.

I like her hair, which I'm pretty sure she cut herself. It sticks out of her head in tufts and bursts that no one could have planned.

"They're gonna have me play some chords on the piano," I tell her. "Sight-read some music. Have me do some vocals. Just prove that I'm generally competent with music, I guess."

♡xoRamona

Do you know those boys who spend all their time trying to cultivate this sad-kid look? You know, floppy hair and lots of sighing? They're all trying to look like this guy. But this guy isn't faking anything. This guy is genuinely, pathetically depressed. It radiates off him. I'm going to get him to smile at least once. I move another seat over so that I'm right next to him.

"But what do you really play?" I ask. "And why are you applying here if they don't have a program for you?" The guy shrugs and mumbles something. "What?" I say.

"I do noise," he says.

"Noise?" This guy is more hardcore than I'd expected.

"Yeah. You've probably heard of a band called Sonic Youth," he says. "They're a rock band that—"

"I know what noise is," I say. I'm annoyed and I let it show in my voice. "Prurient. Merzbow. I was just surprised."

"Oh. Sorry," the guy says. I decide to shrug it off. I'd underestimated him too.

"So that's cool," I say. "Do you have a band?" The guy shakes his head and then shrugs.

"You're actually the first person I've ever met who already knew about Merzbow."

"My school sucks too," I say. "Sam is the only guy at Saint Joe's who knows anything real about music."

"You go to Saint Joseph's Prep?" His expression changes. It's definitely not a smile.

"Not willingly. I'm Ramona, by the way."

"Tom. Sam's your boyfriend?"

"No," I say. "We're friends. Bandmates."

"But that's him that just went in?" Tom motions with his head toward the door.

"Yeah. He plays guitar."

"What kind?"

"Every."

"Every?" And finally Tom kinda smiles. Kinda. I decide it doesn't count. And suddenly I really, really, really want to see this guy smile. Really smile.

"Every," I say. "He plays bass and twelve-string acoustic, and he even owns a sitar."

"Huh. That's cool."

"And a resonator. Anyway, our band's called April and the Rain."

"Is one of you April and the other the Rain?"

I'm surprised that he's the one to make me laugh.

"The name is about springtime, new beginnings and stuff. The rain has to come first."

He nods. "I can dig that," he says.

I feel myself smile again.

Sam

I went into a trance again while I was playing. "Trance" sounds too serious. It's more like I kept playing but I also forgot that I was playing, and I was just listening to the music and not really thinking about anything. And then I remembered that the music was my guitar that I was playing, but luckily it was near the end of the piece.

There were five adults behind this big table. They'd taken some time to make sure they looked official and cold. After I finished, I looked up at them and they nodded.

"Thank you, Mr. Peterson," one woman said in this clipped and crisp voice.

I nodded back and opened my guitar case. They were done making notes now. They were just watching me. It was a little unnerving. I wasn't sure how I did.

"So I'm done? I can go?" I motioned toward the door with my head.

"Yes. Thank you, Mr. Peterson," the woman said again.

As I approached the closed door I heard Ramona's voice on the other side.

"No, no, no, no, no," she was saying. "Prog rock is *not* dead!"

When I opened the door, Ramona and that sad guy were smiling at each other. It took a moment for her to look up at me.

"Sam!" she said. "I found him!" That seemed to confuse this guy as much as it did me. "Wait," she added. "How was your audition? Did you kill? You totally killed, didn't you?"

"Thomas Cogsworthy?" One of the blank faces was standing in the doorway. The other guy stood up and shuffled past me. Ramona was still grinning. I heard the door close behind me.

"I think I did all right," I said. She jumped up and hugged me.

"This is so awesome!" Ramona said in my ear. "We've found our third bandmate, and we're all going to Artibus!"

She smelled nice, but I let her go and took a step back.

"That guy you were just talking to?"

"Yeah, he's totally hardcore. And he does all this experimental stuff, and he can do some vocals for us! You're gonna love him."

"Does he even want to be in our band?"

"Of course he does! I mean, of course he will after we ask him."

I shrugged. Ramona's hard to resist when she's excited. We could talk to the guy. It probably wouldn't work out. Ramona would forget about him by tomorrow.

"Okay," I said. "Let's wait for him." We sat back down. Ramona swung her legs back and forth, singing under her breath.

Really, Ramona is always hard to resist.

Tom

And somehow I'm sitting at a booth in a greasy diner across from two kids who go to the same smarmy private school as Sara. Ramona, the hyperactive spiky-haired girl, is kinda fun. Right now she's drumming on the table with two straws. The guy is probably okay, but he hasn't said much. They were waiting for me after I finished my audition. Apparently this diner is their special place or something.

"Hello again, Janet!" Ramona stops drumming and smiles at the waitress. They order a platter of chili cheese fries to share. I just have a soda, which annoys the waitress, but I don't care.

"So, Tom," Ramona says after Janet leaves us. "Sam and I would like to discuss the prospect of you joining April and the Rain." She's doing this official voice now, kinda like the Artibus people but more friendly, and I can tell it's a bit of a joke. "April and the Rain hasn't quite found its sound yet," she continues.

"We love to experiment. We love tempo changes and polyrhythms. We need someone to do vocals and help us round out our sound. Your extensive knowledge of real music proves that you're not a poseur. Noise could give us the avant-garde edge for which we've been searching. What do you say?" She folds her hands on the table and cocks her head to the side.

"Why don't you go to our website?" Sam says. His voice is so quiet that I barely hear it over the clatter of the diner. "And if you wanna jam sometime, you can let us know."

"Yeah. Cool," I say. The waitress sets my drink and their chili fries down on the table. "So you guys both go to Saint Joseph's Prep?"

"Don't remind us," Ramona says. Sam nods.

"Do you guys know a girl named Sara Miller?"

"Yeah. But not really. She's the class president," Ramona says. Sam kinda nods.

"I used to date her," I say. They both look surprised.

"Oh. She's nice," Ramona says. I can tell by her voice that this is all she has to say about Sara.

"Yeah. I mean, we broke up a few months ago," I say, but I've clearly killed the conversation for now. They eat their chili cheese fries off the same plate without any sort of awkwardness. Their elbows don't bump, they don't get in each other's way, and they don't seem concerned about one person getting more than their share. She said that they weren't a couple. I realize that I'm staring. I take a sip of my soda.

"So what's your website?" I ask. As I expected, they've bought a domain, and it's gonna be so easy to remember that I'm not even going to write it down. But then the Ramona girl pulls out her phone and asks for my number.

"I'll just send you the link right now," she says. Sam keeps eating the fries without looking at us. This girl really wants to me join their band for some reason.

"Yeah, okay," I say.

♡xo Ramona

"He called," I say. I imagine Sam shrugging and switching his phone to his other ear. It's late. He's probably in his room like me, stretched out on his bed.

"Okay, he called," Sam says. "But we don't know if he's any good."

"He's good," I say. "I can tell." And I just know it. Tom is what our band has been missing.

"I guess we'll find out," Sam says.

"Yeah. Tomorrow," I say. "I gave him directions to your place already."

"We don't practice on Tuesdays."

"We do when we're auditioning a new band member."

Sam laughs and probably rolls his eyes.

"Oh yeah," he says. "How could I forget that?"

April and the Rain practices in Sam's mother's garage. Their house has a three-car garage, but since Sam's dad left, there are only two cars, so we have lots of room. Griselda lives there. Griselda is my kit. Sam keeps all of his guitars in his room, and he just brings down whichever one or two he thinks he might want to play that day. His dad is the one who keeps buying the guitars.

I bought Griselda from this girl at school who got it for her birthday and then lost interest in drumming. Griselda is six pieces of awesome in rainbow sparkles. Each drum is a different color, but like, the purple tom has a bunch of different splotches of purple glitter, and the blue bass is a bunch of different blues. It took so many bottles of glitter nail polish, but the result is worth it.

Anyway.

I'm practicing fills when Sam comes into the garage. He's got the neck of his old Fender electric in one hand and his amp in the other. I hit the high hat dramatically.

"I was thinking we should do something in five-four. Or maybe seven-eight."

"Yeah, maybe," Sam says. "What time did he say he was gonna get here?"

"Afternoon," I say.

"That's not a time."

"I know. But that's what he said. Let's just play."

I tap out a starting tempo and Sam plugs in his amp.

⸙

If it wasn't for Sam and the band, I would have gone crazy years ago.

I've made it clear that high school is an abysmal den of idiocy, right?

The summer before my freshman year, they filmed some scenes for a horror movie on our campus. The movie was about Catholic schoolgirls who conjure up a demon. Bloody hijinks ensue. Dad took me to the set on the day that they were filming a chase scene down the long hallway in the English department. They had all these screens up so that it would look like night, and this twentysomething woman ran down the shadowy hall in a really short plaid skirt. And everybody acted like this was really important stuff that they were doing, like her fake screams actually mattered.

It turned out that real high school was about the same: a little bit dark and scary, but mostly just stupid, with fake emotions and everybody taking it all way too seriously.

And I really do have to wear a plaid skirt.

Part of the way through sophomore year, I started wearing Sam's extra blue tie to classes, and there was a big fuss about it. I won that one because the school board got scared that I would come out of the closet as a something or other and they would get sued for discrimination. And then all the other girls started wearing their boyfriend's ties like it was this cool, rebellious thing to do, but they never got called to the principal's office for it.

I don't wear ties to school anymore. Tom's ex-girlfriend, Sara Miller, doesn't either. She's not the type to go for pseudo-rebellion. She's more of the actually-fits-in-without-trying type, the rare sort of person who genuinely likes what's popular and never gets annoyed when other people like the same stuff. She's nice, I guess. She's always pushing some kind of charity through school government, so that's cool.

Anyway.

Tom looks uncomfortable when he finally shows up to band practice. I'm sitting behind Griselda when he comes in with Sam's mom. Sam's mom is weird. She brings us ginger-glazed edamame, which means she's still in her ethnic food phase. Hippie Sam's mom brought us homemade hummus-and-vegetable platters. When she was artsy Sam's mom, she ignored us and played opera really loud.

"Your friend Tom is here," she says.

"Thanks, Mom," Sam says. He takes the tray from her, and she flashes a smile at all of us before leaving.

"So, hey," I say.

"Hey," Tom says. He shifts his weight from one foot to the other and sets the giant amp he's carrying down on the floor. "I like your kit. Glitter is underrated." I knew he would appreciate Griselda. The guy has the most hideous and wonderful car I've ever seen.

"What's that?" I point at the thing in his left hand, this black box with buttons. Tom mumbles something that sounds like "chaos maker" and I say, "Oh cool." Sam turns his back to us and sets the edamame down on the built-in workbench that no one has ever used.

"Is there a place I can plug this in?" Tom says. Sam shows Tom the surge protector his own amp is plugged into. Tom kneels down and starts to get set up. Sam and I meet eyes. He's still doubtful.

"So, Tom," I say, "what were you thinking we should do?"

Sam

Tom was plugging in what looked like a set of guitar pedals without a guitar. He looked up at Ramona and then at me.

"You know that video you guys posted last week?" he said. "I came up with something that I think would sound cool with that, if you wanna mess around with it."

I shrugged.

"Sure," Ramona said. She played a drumroll and I headed over to my guitar and put it back on. I turned my back to them and strummed the high E string. Behind me I heard Ramona start to swing into the song's tempo.

I try as hard as I can to not watch Ramona when she's playing. I mean, it's not possible to never look at her, because so much of playing together is about communicating without talking. But I try to look at Ramona as little as I can.

Ramona is really talented. And determined.

She doesn't care when playing makes her sweaty and messes up her hair.

And she makes these faces.

I was saved from remembering some specific times I've seen Ramona during practice by a noise behind me. It was like wind chimes. Alien wind chimes from a robot planet. I looked over my shoulder. Tom was bent over the pedals and the chaos something. He was making this haunting electronic sound. I could hear where my guitar would fit in. I started the opening chords for the song. I closed my eyes and focused on Ramona's drumming. My body began to move with the time she set. The sound of her stick striking the tom hit my back again and again.

Ramona.

Whenever Ramona eats candy, she arranges it by color first. It's not like an obsessive-compulsive thing. She just thinks it's fun. She usually doesn't like anything orange, so she often gives those to me. Greens are her favorites.

Her sneeze is really weird. She scrunches up her face and makes a noise like a tiny snort. It's like she's trying to stop the sneeze from getting away.

Ramona's mother started giving her piano lessons when she was four. She died when Ramona was nine, and her father hired someone from the academy to give her lessons after that. She still has private lessons, and she never talks about her mother.

We like to watch really bad shows together so we can make fun of the dialogue. Shows about psychics solving crimes are the most fun. Ramona is really good at predicting what the psychics will say next.

Ramona can't stand people who put up a false front. "Poseur" is her darkest insult.

She's fun, and she's real.

Ramona's an assertive girl, and if she was into me as more than a friend, she would have just said so a long time ago. She's trusted me with her friendship, and I'm not going to ever put that at risk.

I turned around.

From over her kit, Ramona met my eyes. She grinned and bit her lip. We sounded good. Tom filled out the song without drowning either of us out. I could tell the guy knows what he's doing. Ramona played a fill, closed her eyes, and threw her head back.

I turned away again.

After we ran through the song a second time, we all sat down on the garage floor and ate the stuff Mom brought. Ramona hadn't stopped talking since she got out from behind her drums.

"We need to consider doing something with that song we were working on sophomore year. Do you remember? You played like a da-da-dum de-da?"

I nodded. Tom looked amused, which was a good sign. Some people find Ramona overwhelming, and after our first practice, she's going to be even more adamant that he join the band.

We had a really awesome jam with him. Toward the end Tom had started musing about and humming some lyrics, and it sounded like he has an okay voice. I didn't have any expectations for Tom. I had no idea if he would be any good at all. Ramona claimed she could tell just from their conversation in the basement hall that he was a real musician and that he was destined to be our third band member.

She was right about him being a real musician.

"You should come to our Saturday practice," I said to Tom. Ramona grinned at me.

Tom

I'm feeling better than I've felt in weeks. I'm not saying I feel great; I just feel better. My car needs Freon, but the evening is cool and it's nice driving home with the windows down. The glitter on my hood is red, and I remember Ramona hitting her high hat and bouncing in her seat.

Ramona is fun and funny. Sam is a good musician and a nice enough guy. It was good to forget about Sara and everything else for a while. I'm gonna go back for another practice this weekend.

(I realize that I actually do want to be in their band.)

I'd gone to their website and been surprised. They were doing some cool stuff with only two people. Mom's always bugging me about making friends, so I figured I'd give it a try.

Right now it's almost dinnertime, and the rich neighborhood in the city is half an hour from my parents' house in Ferguson. On the highway with the windows down, the car is thunderous. Ominous. It's a small, chaotic world. I wish there were some way I could record this wind and be able to capture this feeling of small space. I might see if I can make something on the synth that has a similar feel.

> (Ramona would do supplementary fills and tempo
> changes,
> amping up the drama.
> I don't know what Sam would do—something
> amazing
> that I would never think of
> that completes the piece
> and makes it
> a song.)

I get home before six thirty, so I'm not late. Mom is setting the table though, and Dad is already in the kitchen.

When I come in, Mom gives me this look, like she's annoyed with me just for making her think that I might be late. I was one of those "I thought it was menopause but actually I was pregnant" babies. I grew up listening to my mother joke about how after raising three boys she thought she was almost done with parenting—and then I came along.

We sit down at the table and my dad calls me "Champ"

and asks about my day. He called my older brothers "Champ" when they were kids. They were the kind of boys you would call "Champ." They liked sports and wanted to learn how to fix cars instead of paint them with glitter.

"It was fine, Pops," I say.

My parents and I have this nightly dinner ritual where they try to get me to talk. Some nights I don't have much to say. (Okay, most nights. I just don't like sharing my feelings. They're mine.) The whole thing just seems so forced to me. Maybe if they just let me eat in silence one night, then I'd feel like talking the next.

"Your father and I were planning on going to Gran's lake house this weekend," Mom says. I barely suppress a groan. Gran left the house to Mom and her sister. It has terrible air-conditioning and no Internet.

"Do we have to?" I ask. "I kinda have plans."

"Actually, we were thinking that you could stay home this time," she says. "We think you can handle yourself for a few days."

"Really?" I look up from my plate at them.

"No parties," Mom says. "And no public art projects." (Last year the glitter bombing of a fire hydrant resulted in a visit from the St. Louis County PD. Ever since then I've been more discreet. With Glitter in Odd Places, that is. They never connected the fountain to me.)

"And no girls," Dad adds. He laughs, so I guess that's supposed to be funny.

"Yeah, okay," I say. "Thanks, guys."

"What plans do you have?" Mom asks.

"I met some kids at the Artibus thing," I say. "We're gonna get together and jam." Mom looks thrilled; she thinks I need friends. She asks the questions parents ask, and I recite for her Ramona's and Sam's stats. The fact that they attend Saint Joe's impresses Mom, just like it did with Sara. After I'm done eating, I'm able to escape by pleading the demands of my summer reading list.

Pretty typical night, but like I said before, I'm feeling a little better. Up in my room, I wonder if Ramona would ever want to go glitter bombing with me. Based on her drum kit, I think she might.

♡x Ramona

It should come as no surprise to you that I have a nemesis. Her name is Emmalyn. Emmalyn Evans, which to me sounds like the name of a character in a children's book. Emmalyn Evans, go to the store. Emmalyn Evans, shut the damn door.

Anyway, she started it.

First semester freshman year, we had nearly every class together. Two months into my high school career, the plaid uniforms were already driving me crazy. So I cut my hair. And I mean, *I* cut my hair. In the bathroom, with scissors from Dad's desk. My hair was supposed to be jagged and uneven. I was trying to look like a mess, and I loved it.

When I walked into my first class that morning, Emmalyn gasped out loud and squeaked, "Oh my God, what happened to you?"

So I rolled my eyes and said, "Obviously nothing that I didn't want to happen. I'm not a sheeple like you." Everybody laughed, and Tony Smith went, "Baaaa."

From then on, everything I did was subject to Emmalyn Evans's disdain. And it wasn't just about my hair. If I answered a teacher's question wrong, she snickered. If we played dodgeball in gym, she targeted me. The first time I was called to the principal's office for wearing Sam's tie, Emmalyn said in a loud whisper, "She's always trying to get attention, isn't she?"

Over the past four years, I've continued to cut, braid, grow out, and shave different sections of my hair however I've pleased.

Every semester I have had at least three classes with Emmalyn. I had this dumb hope that maybe this year I would see a little less of her, but apparently the universe needs us working against each other to keep its balance, because for senior year, Emmalyn Evans is in my homeroom.

On the first day of school, when she walked in the room and saw me, she sighed in this resigned way, as if I followed her there or something. I was tapping a five-four beat on my desk with my index fingers. I knew from previous years that my desk drumming annoys her, or at least she likes to pretend it annoys her. Here's the thing: she always sits near me. Not right by me, but near me. I guess so that I can overhear all her snide comments and smug giggles.

I wanted Emmalyn to know that if she was gonna pull that move in homeroom, then she was gonna have to deal with me tapping out beats and fills every morning, so I played louder. Emmalyn sat down in the row next to me, two desks ahead, even though there were plenty of empty seats farther away.

It's like she wanted me to get on her nerves.

I tapped louder on the desk. Em-Uh-Lin EV-ans.

She sighed loudly again. As she flipped her hair over her shoulder, she turned to give me a quick glare. I rolled my eyes.

Emmalyn Evans, she's such a bore. Emmalyn Evans, she's always sore.

One more school year and I'm done with this place.

It was important to Dad that I attended Saint Joe's. He's been teaching here for almost thirty years. He's old. Like, actually old, not regular-parents old. He was fifty when I was born. My mother was forty. They thought that they couldn't have kids.

Anyway, being a single parent with a teacher's salary and all, Dad was really proud that I'd at least get the best possible education. Saint Joseph's Preparatory is a little bit famous, and a lot of the graduates go on to Ivy League universities. So, yeah, I know I'm lucky that I get to go to school tuition free, but that doesn't mean there isn't a cost.

My classmates think that having certain names on the soles of their shoes is a personal achievement for which they should be admired. As if they have these shoes not because of their parents' money, but because they earned them by being intrinsically better beings.

Consequently, most of the conversations that I overhear in the girl's bathroom exasperate me. Someone's new lake house being in the wrong neighborhood is what passes for juicy gossip around here. A scandal is when a purse turns out to be a knockoff.

Thank God for Sam. He's so different from all of them that it's like he's from another planet. While I find our classmates insufferably annoying, Sam finds them utterly baffling.

Thankfully, Sam and I have the same lunch period and we were able to snag a picnic table in the courtyard to sit at. Well, Sam is sitting at it, and I'm sitting on it, next to his sandwich.

"In bio, I was in a group lab with Kaylie Rushton and Pam Jones, and instead of helping me with the microscope, they recited for each other the outfits they wore to every party all summer. Why?"

"Why what?" I say.

"Why did they do that? Do they actually care what the other girl wore back in July?"

"Nah," I say. "They just wanted to talk about what they wore back in July."

"Why?" Sam asks.

I love you so much, I think.

"It's only the third day back, Sammy-Oh. Gimme a break," I say.

"Hey, you spent twenty minutes talking about Emmalyn glaring at you in homeroom."

"Yeah, but I didn't demand an explanation for her behavior. You must learn to be at peace with the alien motivations of girls with fluff for brains."

Sam shrugs and picks up his sandwich.

"I just can't comprehend that level of superficiality existing." He takes a big bite, and mustard drips on his chin.

I love you so much, I think.

Sam

Mr. Van Bueran is the guidance counselor at Saint Joe's. His voice is a deep baritone, and he clears his throat a lot. Ramona once compared him to a living tuba, which I know sounds mean, but if you met him, you'd understand.

He took an interest in me after Dad left sophomore year. He would call me into his office once every few weeks to remind me that he was there for me if I ever needed to talk. But I didn't need to talk. Dad's moving out was pretty okay with me. That meant we didn't have to pretend anymore. I didn't tell Van Bueran though; I just told him that I thought I was adjusting well.

He still had me come by from time to time just to "catch up," and I continued to be well adjusted. Then last winter he said, "So you must be getting excited about applying to Artibus next year, huh?"

I said, "Yeah, kinda."

And his face brightened.

"Why only 'kind of' excited?" he asked.

He'd somehow found the only thing I needed to talk to somebody about.

I was having doubts about Artibus.

So it wasn't a surprise when I was called to his office on the second day of school.

"Hey, Sam," he said to me. "How was your summer?"

"Good," I said. I sat down in the chair across from his desk.

"Artibus had their evaluations recently, didn't they?" Mr. Van Bueran said. He leaned back in his chair and regarded me.

"Yeah," I said. "I think I did well."

"That's great," Van Bueran said. He was using this slow cautious voice, like he was worried that I'd bolt if he pressed too hard. "Are you still wondering if a chemistry major would be a better fit for you? Are you still feeling passionate about sustainable products?"

"Yeah," I said. When I heard my own voice, I got why he was worried I'd bolt.

It's hard for me to admit that maybe I don't want music to be my whole life.

Music is Ramona's life.

Music is what brought Ramona into my life.

"Saint Louis University has a great chemistry program," Van Bueran said. "Have you checked it out?"

I shook my head.

He smiled and reached into his desk drawer. He handed me SLU's pamphlet. Everyone on the cover looked like they had made all the right decisions.

"SLU would set you up to get into a top-tier grad program," he said.

I shrugged.

"You should think about it," he said.

I nodded.

I don't talk much, but when I do, Ramona takes the time to listen. Every once in a while, I get mad at Dad for taking off the way he did and continuing to be only marginally interested in me. There isn't anybody I ever wanted to talk about that stuff with but Ramona.

And one day in the garage she said to me, "Look, Sammy-Oh, maybe this is all your dad is giving you because this is all that he *can* give. Maybe your dad just isn't capable of emotionally supportive relationships. It's sad, but there are people out there like that. It's shit luck that one of those people is your dad, but I bet it's a lot worse to actually *be* him."

I thought about it, and I realized that it was true.

The man has no friends. He left his wife because she hated him for never opening up to her. He doesn't know what to do with his son, so he spends money and retreats.

As I thought about it, I realized that it was less harmful to feel sorry for someone than to be angry with him. I realized that I can't change who my dad is.

And I never would have realized these things without Ramona.

How can I disappoint her after all the plans she's made?

Tom

When I was a freshman, the seniors looked so old. Now the freshmen look so young. But really, that's the only thing that's different. Everything else in this place is exactly the same.

The populars congregate in the courtyard before classes. Outcasts are restricted to the cafeteria year-round. Sports teams hang out by the gym doors as if they can't wait to get inside. I'm still sitting with my back against the south wall near all the kids that want to be seen as "different."

I'm friendly with lots of people here, but I don't have a group. People invite me to parties and sometimes I go, but I'm not really a part of their planet. I'm like a satellite friend.

I like to sit near (but not with) the theater nerds, because they tend to have the best conversations. Today is the first day of school though, so Ally is holding a semiofficial meeting about play selections for the year.

I went out with Ally Tabor for a few weeks sophomore year—because she asked me to, and I figured I was supposed to say yes. I didn't mind when she broke it off, and we're decently good friends, I guess. Ally's real name is Alejandra. She's the kind of girl who is always inventing new ways to do her heavy eyeliner. She bites her nails, but when she paints them, they're always black. (She may have been using the same bottle of nail polish since middle school.) Ally takes her drama club presidency very seriously, and I like that about her.

Right now she is sitting cross-legged with the rest of the theater nerds circled around her.

"If we time a performance of *Death of a Salesman* right, we'll have at least half of the sophomore class attending to get out of reading it for American lit," she's saying. "And this year's lazy sophomore may become next year's junior theater fan."

The others all nod at her wisdom. In the last couple of minutes, a few freshmen in all black have come up to the edge of the group. They nod too, looking at the others as if asking for permission to participate.

Three yards to the right of me, the kids that think they're vampires or something are arguing over who owes who a cigarette. I also have a view of the guys who play boring generic rock and think they're edgy musicians. I try not to overhear their conversations; whenever I do, it makes me cringe.

I turn my music back on and lean against the wall. Nothing has changed. No one out here is hoping I'll say hey to them. No one out here is doing anything I want to participate in. Here's how to survive high school: find a safe place and then just keep your head down and wait it out.

♡ to Ramona

Wednesday after school, I don't go over to Sam's house like I do most days. When I get home, I drop my bag by the door and head straight to the piano in the front room and sit down. It's an old upright, but it belonged to my mom and we've taken good care of it.

John, my piano instructor, has me running all the scales over again at faster and faster tempos each time. I'm on C scales right now.

It. Is. Boring. As. Fucking. Hell.

c.d.e.f.g.a.b.

c.d.e.f.g.a.b.

c.d.e.f.g.a.b.

But if I can't run the C scale with the metronome set to 150 when John comes over tomorrow afternoon, then he might mention it in front of my dad, and Dad already said something yesterday about all the extra band practice cutting into my piano time.

Dad takes my piano lessons as seriously as he takes school grades. He pays for my lessons out of Mom's life insurance money, and he's really supportive about me wanting to go to Artibus. Lots of parents would want their kid to pursue a more practical career, but Dad wants me to be a pianist like Mom.

Dad's not a musician at all, but he's still pretty cool. For a dad, I mean. Especially an old dad. He likes it when I argue with him about politics. He always says that not enough teachers encourage teenagers to think for themselves. He even stood up for me during the whole tie drama—and don't forget, the principal at St Joe's is my dad's boss.

I guess we are closer than a lot of other kids and their parents. I mean, it's just us two at home.

So I'm gonna go to Artibus with Sam, and I'll study piano there. John says I'm good enough to have a career, if I follow his instructions and practice hard.

c.d.e.f.g.a.b.

c.d.e.f.g.a.b.

Sam

It's been weird having Tom around all the time. Ramona always wants to know what Tom thinks about this song or argues with him about that band, and I like to sit and listen to people talk—especially Ramona—but in the past week, I've been missing when it was just her and me.

But today in Tom's car, Ramona was delivering her "Yes Is Philosophically and Scientifically the Greatest Band in Recorded History" speech. She'd just finished her in-depth comparison of Bill Bruford and Alan White when Tom interrupted her.

"'Owner of a Lonely Heart.'"

"What?" It's rare to be able to stop the thought train that is Ramona's mind, but Tom had done it swiftly and without looking up from the road.

"'Owner of a Lonely Heart' is a glaring blister of a flaw on Yes's permanent record. It's musical blasphemy," he replied.

"It's awesomely bad."

"Yes, it is awe inspiring how bad it is, but that's not a

point in their favor. They were trying to make a *good* song, and they failed. There is no other way to look at it."

Ramona opened her mouth.

"He's right," I said. "They're one of the best bands in history, but even good bands sucked in the eighties."

"Well," Ramona said and fell silent.

Silent.

Ramona fell silent.

And I had to admit that it was kind of satisfying, 'cause "Owner of a Lonely Heart" is a terrible song.

And then she laughed and said, "All right, I'll concede that point."

And I realized that maybe Tom was good for us.

It's good for Ramona to have someone to pull the rug out from under her every once and awhile.

She turned and smiled at me.

And I realized that it's probably good for me to have another person between me and Ramona.

Tom

All around me, I see wasted opportunities.

Blank concrete walls, light posts, corner trash cans—if someone comes along and makes these things better looking, makes them art, why is that illegal?

Sure, beauty is in the eye of the beholder, but there is a clear difference between art and gang tags or hate crimes.

At least there sure as hell is a difference between gang tags and Glitter in Odd Places. In the past eighteen months I've coated thirty-three pens on chains (they're soon to be extinct) with silver or gold glitter. I've painted four fast-food restaurants' talk boxes blue, green, pink, and peach. I covered three city sidewalk squares in three vastly different neighborhoods with two inches of Call Me Crazy multicolored sparkles purchased from my favorite craft store, Grift Craft. (Yeah, I have a favorite craft store. Deal with it.)

And I glitter bombed one fire hydrant.

(I knew that this would be crossing a line, but I felt that

it was time. It was a tactical decision. And I was feeling confident. Sara and I had been together for five months. She got GOP, and she got me—and it was so amazing to have someone who understood me.)

For public safety, I matched the glitter to the hydrant's original red and yellow, and I was careful not to get glitter or glue in the hinges. (It's very important to me that my art never causes harm.) After I was done, the fire hydrant looked and would function exactly the same as before, except that it was glittery.

And why not? Why can't these things that we have to have—these fire hydrants and traffic lights and bus stops and overhead passes—why can't they be beautiful and unique, or at least interesting to look at? We have people who want do it for us for free, people who don't think art should only be locked up in galleries.

It's at least something worth thinking about, right?

So anyway, I was proud of my fire hydrant.

The city of St. Louis didn't exactly feel the same way.

The cop showed up during dinner, good timing on his part.

Mom and I were still at the table when Dad called my name. By his voice, I knew something was up.

The cop's badge said "Smith."

His face said "grave concern."

Smith asked me, "Son, is this your car?" and he handed me a still shot from a security camera. It showed my car in the alley next to the fire hydrant.

"Yes, sir," I said. I had imagined a moment like this, and I was determined to go out with dignity.

"Mr. Cogsworthy," Officer Smith said. (I hate, hate, hate it when adults call me Mr., as if they were treating me with respect when actually they mean the opposite by it.) "Is it a coincidence that your car, which is covered in glitter, was seen on camera near a piece of city property that was vandalized by glitter?"

And I couldn't help it.

I laughed.

I laughed in front of Officer Smith and my parents, because "vandalized by glitter" was the funniest phrase I had ever heard spoken aloud in such a serious voice.

I'm gonna make a long story short and say that in the end I was really lucky. I was technically arrested, though I never actually left my parents' home, and I went before a judge and read the statement of apology that my mom wrote, instead of the artistic manifesto that I'd prepared. The judge was lenient because he said that he had a grandson who was "like me" (I'm not even gonna comment on that one), and I did sixteen hours of community service cleaning up gang tags in bad neighborhoods.

I was also grounded for two months, and Mom and Dad have definitely kept the leash tighter since then.

The worst part was that Sara didn't want me to do GOP anymore. And that was when we started fighting.

♡✗Ramona

"Here's the thing about Neil Peart," I explain to the guys. "He knows that acoustic drums will always be the soul of percussion, but he embraces the innovations allowed by electronic drums."

It's a normal afternoon in Sam's garage. We're taking a quick break before we try to record our new song. Today Tom brought his touch-pad chaos thing, usual collection of pedals, and a didgeridoo he made out of PVC pipe. We just messed around for a little while, and it didn't take long for a song to emerge. The music we make with Tom is strange and exciting. It isn't always technically difficult, but it's always new.

The song we wrote today opens with the lone, low tones of the didgeridoo, then Sam comes in with this crazy riff on the authentic sitar his dad brought back from India. Just as I come in with the polyrhythmic beat, Tom switches from the real didgeridoo to a premade recording he runs effects through, and Sam begins lead melody on the electric guitar.

The setup for all of this is ridiculous. Instruments, pedals, and cables are all over the floor, and Sam had to get another extension cord. Because of the clutter, we're all standing or sitting behind our instruments.

"Electronic drums were invented by the guy from Moody Blues," Tom says. "They deserve a place in any true percussionist's heart. And a band without a true percussionist brain cannot transcend this realm."

"We don't have that problem," Sam says.

"Thanks," I say, "but I don't think I deserve the compliment. I'm a good drummer, yeah, but I'm not that innovative."

"Remember just the other day when you were saying how much you liked the sound when you drummed on the garage floor?" Tom says. "Why haven't you ever recorded it for a song?"

Something inside me clicks into place.

"You already treat the whole world like your drum set anyway," Sam says. "We might as well start incorporating that in the band."

My chest feels good, like suddenly my lungs have more room. I think of the sound of drumming on my desk, Sam's steering wheel, my piano stool. I remember the tones of my sticks hitting concrete and plastic, hollow wood and thick, dark asphalt.

It never occurred to me that maybe I was making

real music

that other people would like too.

And to think I might have not spoken to Tom that first day.

Sam

My mother is an adult who has never figured herself out and probably never will.

When my parents met, my mother was switching from a theater major to social work. She dropped out of college when she married my father.

When I was small, my mother was always trying to find a different sport for me, a new activity. Pottery, capoeira, children's theater. When I was eleven, I told her that I didn't want to try anything new anymore. I just wanted to keep taking guitar lessons.

In the final six months of the last presidential election, she became opinionated and involved. She spoke at meetings and bought me clever campaign shirts. She walked neighborhoods registering people to vote. She talked about running for local government, about making a difference through democracy. Her candidate lost. She never talks about politics anymore.

Just before the divorce was finalized, Mom started

mentioning that she had always been a deeply spiritual person. She started doing yoga and wore bracelets with magnets and bells on them. For a while she talked about past lives and energy fields, but that tapered off. Some weekends she still does yoga, but recently she's been watching cooking shows and trying the recipes out. It's way more fun now that she's past the herbal-drinks phase.

But I still have my guitars and band practice.

I love my mother. I have more respect for her than I do my father.

But I also know that I don't want to be like her.

I love music. I love playing my guitars.

But I don't love it enough to want to put myself through what it takes to become a professional musician.

Music will always be a part of my life. A huge part.

But there are other things in life that I also want, and I don't want to give them up to pursue just that one thing.

I want to make the world a better place, to help the environment.

And I really like chemistry. A lot.

Music will be always be a part of my life. A huge part.

But I'm not cut out for the musician's life.

I know myself well enough to know that.

Tom

Just before we broke up, Sara and I had a fight about goldfish.

I had a brilliant plan, and she objected to it on ethical grounds.

It was late last spring, toward the end I guess. After school I drove to Juan's Pet Supply and Fish Emporium to buy goldfish, the tiny kind that aren't pets but actually pet food. (Why would anyone want a pet fish that eats other fish? Isn't that both creepy and a lot of work?)

Fish like that cost about ten cents. I spent twenty bucks. Then I drove across the city to pick up Sara. She'd stayed late at Saint Joe's for a student government meeting. Whenever I picked Sara up there, I never actually drove into the campus. I just parked by the gates. She didn't seem to mind.

"Have I ever got a date planned for us, kiddo," I told her as she climbed in my car.

"Really?" she said. She reached behind her head with

both hands and tightened her ponytail. I'd drawn a picture of her in my journal with her hands behind her head like that.

"Oh yeah," I said. "This is gonna blow your mind." I jerked my head toward the backseat. Sara gasped when she saw the bags of goldfish.

"What—"

"Just wait," I told her, and I drove us to downtown St. Louis. There's a massive fountain downtown, all adorned with these wanton warrior mermaids. That fountain was our destination.

I parked a few blocks away, and before we got out of the car, I stuck one of my dad's baseball caps on my head, the brim pulled down low over my face. I handed Sara one of the goldfish bags and we walked across the square together.

"This is the first in a series of sister projects to Glitter in Odd Places," I told her, "I'm gonna call it something like 'Surprise! Real Life!'"

When we reached the fountain, I tore open the first bag and poured the fish into the fountain.

The fish kinda freaked out for a moment, but then they slowed down and started swimming in circles like in the pet shop. It looked awesome.

I poured in the second and third.

Compared to these tiny, real fish, the mermaids looked crazed.

I turned to Sara and reached for the last bag. For a moment she wouldn't let it go. I thought she was just nervous. Some people across the street were looking at us. I pulled the bag from her hands and released the last of the fish. Then I took out my phone, snapped a quick picture, and grabbed Sara's arm as I turned away. We jogged together back to the car, and I started the engine as soon as I'd closed the door.

"It's gonna look even more awesome tomorrow," I said. "After they're all dead, it's gonna be so gruesome. Like the goldfish have been sacrificed to the false idol fishes."

"But you're the one who's killed them," Sara said. I glanced away from the road to look at her. She had her arms crossed over her chest defensively, and I couldn't recognize the look on her face.

"They were gonna die anyway," I said. "They're fish food."

"They're living creatures," she said. "Isn't that the point of your art project?"

"You eat meat," I said.

"That's not the point," she said. Her arms were crossed in front of her chest, and her lower lip stuck out.

"What is the point?"

She didn't say anything, so I didn't either. I drove her home without asking first. Before she got out of the car, she turned back to me.

"The point is, you shouldn't be doing this stuff anymore, Tom. You got arrested! I know you're really passionate about your art and your music and all that, but maybe I'd like to go on a real date sometime," she said. "One where you actually treat me like a girlfriend." And then, before I could say anything, she slammed the door.

The next day was Saturday. On Sunday I called her and acted like nothing had happened, and to my relief, so did she.

A week later I read an article in the *Post Dispatch* that said a "prank" had cost the city five thousand dollars to fix when the filter system of a downtown fountain became clogged with goldfish. This scared me to death because I was still on probation, and it did really upset me. Causing real harm goes against my ethics.

I was gonna tell Sara about it and admit that maybe I should have thought things through more, but before I got a chance, she broke up with me.

I don't really want to go over that conversation.

♡xoRamona

My pulse is racing.

Sam's garage is a concert hall for the most kick-ass, avant-garde, in-your-face experimental noise rock band on the planet. Over the sound of my breathing, I hear the drone of Sam's guitar coming to its close. There is a moment of silence, and in my head the audience is screaming.

We just played the best we ever have together. I glance over at Sam. He has that slow, sweet smile creeping across his face.

"Guys," I say, "we are the future classical musicians."

Tom laughs. And he has a nice laugh. Tom is pretty cute when he's not moping. Which he's been doing a lot less lately.

Sam crosses the room and saves our recording on the laptop.

"I think we're ready for Nanami to hear our new sound," he says. "Besides, she posted yesterday asking why we hadn't loaded a song or video lately."

"Agreed," I say. I move out from behind Griselda and lie down on the cool concrete floor.

"Who's Nanami?" Tom says.

"Nanami is our fan," I explain. "And if she doesn't like you, then we'll just have to get a new fan."

"If she has a critique, we should at least listen," Sam says. He sits down next to me. "She's been loyal for a long time." He puts his hand down absentmindedly, and it's kind of by my head, brushing my hair. I pretend that he's wishing he could stroke it.

"But she's gonna love ya, Tom," I say. "I can feel it."

"You 'feel' things a lot." He sits down on the other side of me.

"I'm always right."

"She's often right," Sam says.

Tom smiles, bigger than I've ever seen him smile before. I know that Tom likes being in the band with us. He doesn't talk about other people often, so I'm not sure that he has any other friends.

"Okay. We take a short rest, Sam does a fast mix on the song, and then we upload it."

"Cool," Sam says.

"I guess this makes you official, Tom," I say.

"I thought I already was official. We're been practicing together for a month."

"You're Nanami official now," I say. "That's a whole new security level. I might let you name the next song."

"But not this one," Sam says. I immediately sit up on my elbows. Sam doesn't speak up like this very often. "I thought of a title while we were playing."

In Sam's room I sit on the end of his bed and bounce while the boys lean over the desk. Sam's room is cool. When his mom was in her interior-decorating phase, she hung all of his guitars on the wall. It's doubly cool because not only does it look killer, but it's convenient.

"You're gonna break my bed," Sam says over his shoulder.

On my next bounce, I jump up and hop over to Sam's desk. "Deadly Moving Pieces" has finished uploading. Sam is typing out what he always does, "Samuel Peterson—Guitar, Ramona Andrews—Drums," and then he adds "Tom Cogsworthy—Chaos Maker."

"What?" Tom says. "I mean, that's awesome, but what does it mean?"

"Isn't that your thing?" I ask. "Your chaos maker, the synth with the buttons and the touch pad?"

"Kaosolator, with a K." He spells it out for Sam. "But I like chaos maker."

In the end Sam lists him as "Tom 'Chaos Maker' Cogsworthy—Kaosolator."

Tom laughs. It's starting to be a sound that I like very much.

Sam

Ramona and I kind of went on a date once. Kinda.

She'd suddenly decided that we should go to at least one homecoming dance.

"It will be awful, and we'll leave early and go do something cool," she said. "But we're in high school, and we should at least be able to say that we went to one dance."

So we went.

Ramona wore a short blue dress and made her hair stand up all pretty with glittery gel. I got her a corsage, which surprised her, but I thought that it was what I was supposed to do. It was two white roses. She still has it on her bookshelf in her room.

After we'd skipped out on the dance, we drove to Lambert Airport and watched the planes taking off and landing. We sat on the hood of the car and leaned back against the windshield. It was cool out, even for fall, and we wore our regular jackets with our formal stuff. Ramona talked about our school and all the kids with messed-up priorities. And we talked about how people become the people that they are and whether any of us can ever escape that.

Ramona said, "Sometimes the whole world seems like this big machine churning people out, making everyone into the sort of person they're expected to be. It scares me.

"I can feel it pulling at me sometimes, telling me to take the easier route, to stop trying so hard to be myself, to only try for the simple things in life. And it never stops. The machine can catch you at any age. No one is too old to sell out." Then she turned to look at me, and she had this hopeful look on her face like maybe I could make her be less afraid.

And I wanted to grab her and tell her that she was the most unique and interesting person I had ever met. That I thought she was brave and funny and was going to make amazing music that changed the world. And to kiss her. I wanted that most of all.

And I almost did. I really did consider it.

But what I said was, "I think that as long as you can still see the machine, then you stand a chance of outrunning it."

She smiled then. I think it was the right thing to say.

Right thing to do.

If she had wanted to kiss me, she would have done it herself.

Tom

"So here's the plan," I say.

I am taking Ramona glitter bombing.

"What we are about to do is technically illegal," I say.

To certain authority figures, everything we are about to do is completely illegal.

"We're going to walk through this parking lot like we're just taking a shortcut. When we get to the fence, we're going to glitter bomb. We aren't going to talk about it. We're going to do it quickly. Then we're going to walk away."

I'm holding a greasy fast-food bag. We already ate the burgers.

The bag has two pots of rubber cement and three bottles of glitter.

Ramona is wearing a black turtleneck, like we are spies in a movie.

Actually, her school uniform would have provided us the

kind of cover we could use in this operation, but I didn't mention it.

We're crossing the parking lot, just the two of us, on a Thursday. Band practice was canceled on account of Sam's head cold, which Ramona described as "plague-esque."

We reach a broken chain-link fence leaning against a trash tree. We're just outside downtown St. Louis in a neighborhood that used to have more money but now isn't the kind of place you would want to be in at night.

There was an elementary school here once. This used to be a hopeful place. Kids used to play here. The city school system has been trying to sell this building for a long time. This corner of the parking lot has been forgotten. The kind of people who would be walking past this fence might be up to no good, or they might just be down on their luck (down on their luck for a long time).

I love going to these parts of the city. I love the old signs and the faded painted murals advertising businesses now long closed. I love the wildflowers that grow in cracks and gutters. I like thinking about the people who used to live and work here.

People thought these buildings would always be busily populated, that this neighborhood would always be kept up. They lived their lives, spent their money, moved on, and died.

For some crazy reason, people always think the world is never going to change. I like to imagine my school steps crumbling, someone wondering about me.

October light is falling in the weeds around us. The concrete beneath our feet is cracked like rivers driving through continents. With the little paintbrush in the rubber cement bottle, I begin to coat the fence. I'm not trying to be neat; that's not the point.

Last week, Ramona asked me about my car. She was lying on the floor of Sam's garage, all sweaty from drumming. Sam had gone to help his mother with something.

"We all spend so much time in our cars. I think it's weird that more people don't feel compelled to decorate their cars."

"I get that," Ramona said. "If I had my own car, I would write lyrics all over it. Little drawings too. But doesn't it make you feel weird to be driving a car covered in glitter all across the city?"

"Why not?" I said. "Because you have to admit that you

wouldn't be asking me that if I were a girl. Why is it that one gender gets to own a certain sort of reflective plastic? I think glitter is badass, and I refuse to abide by other people's irrational cultural assumptions."

When I was done talking, Ramona was looking at me strangely. Sara used to look at me like that.

"Take me with you next time you go glitter bombing," she said, just like Sara did.

I was telling someone my real feelings, and they wanted to get to know me better instead of arguing with me.

Terrifying. But just too tempting to resist.

Ramona takes out the light-blue glitter. It's called something like "I'm Just a Dreamer," but Ramona said it should be called something like "I'm Not Really a Stripper." Her hands work behind mine. We don't talk, just like I told her we wouldn't. One slow car drives by us, its driver absorbed in a phone conversation. The windshield catches the sun and sends glare into my eyes.

Ramona works quickly, and before long, we have covered a patch of fence roughly six feet in diameter. I motion to her. She drops the glitter in the bag and I crumple it closed. We take a step back and look.

We've worked magic in this forgotten schoolyard. The clumps and lumps of glitter are catching that October light, and the fence has been transmuted into a shimmering border between this world scarred by drugs and poverty and another, perhaps better, place.

"That is awesome," Ramona says, "in the old-timey biblical meaning of the word."

I feel the corners of my mouth twitch.

"Come on, kiddo," I say. "We gotta go."

I pick up the paper sack, and we walk away.

♡x♡Ramona

Should I have seen it coming that I have a thing for Tom?

'Cause I didn't expect that.

At all.

He seemed so mopey when we first met.

It was a few weeks before I even thought, "Huh, he's kinda cute."

He thinks a little too highly of synthesized drums.

He still doesn't understand the full importance of progressive rock.

But I guess I'm just a sucker for guys who are unapologetically themselves.

Also, I gave Sam chicken soup today.

While he'd been sick, I'd made the soup, and then I didn't get a chance to give it to him before he got better, so today when he picked me up, I brought the soup with me. And when I told him that it was my mom's recipe, he didn't get all awkward or sentimental on me. He was just like, "So it's like soup from your mom too. Cool."

Which is such a perfect, Sam thing to say.

And he totally didn't get that it was a weird thing to say.

That seems to be the other thing I'm into.

A guy who is super weird and doesn't even know it.

I'm still totally in love with Sam.

And now I've got a killer crush on Tom.

Shit.

Maybe I'm just into guys who make music with me.

Sam

"IS THIS A NEW BAND? I LOVE YOU SO MUCH FOREVER!" said Nanami's message. It was the Friday before Halloween, and we were on my laptop in the garage. Nanami had changed her avatar photo. In this one, she was making a weird fish face with another girl who had anime eyes drawn on her eyelids.

"Huh," Ramona said. "Are we a new band?"

"Yeah," I said. Suddenly it came to me. She and I are April and the Rain, but this is something new. Tom has made us something different. "We need a new name," I said.

"Well, you know what that means," Ramona said.

"Actually, I don't," Tom said.

"Brainstorm party!" Ramona and I said together.

I had bags from the gas station in both hands, so I turned and pushed the front door closed with my foot.

"Over the years Sam and I have determined the exact procedure of loafing that best serves creative brain function," Ramona was saying to Tom in the family room. "Radiohead (obviously), chocolate, garlic popcorn, and here's the curveball—orange soda."

"Surprising."

"But effective. The little nook between the TV and the corner of the couch is where I sit. I will protect that spot with physical force if necessary."

"She isn't joking," I said as I came into the room. "I had a drumstick-shaped bruise on my leg for weeks." I couldn't help the grin on my face. I love how seriously Ramona takes our brainstorm parties and I was enjoying Tom's veneration for the rules.

"I will respect the sanctity of your nook," Tom said. "When do we start?"

"Now," Ramona said. I flopped down on the couch.

Tom

Here's a list of the band names (listed from lame to almost awesome) that we debated at the brainstorm party:

Interstellar Lunch Menu (Ramona)

A Rose Is a Rhododendron (Me)

The Hug Addicts (Ramona, shot down quickly by Sam)

Autoerotic Annunciation (Sam, shot down quickly by Ramona)

Brain Maze (Ramona)

Homemade Atom Bomb (Me)

Feng Shui or Die! (Sam)

Here's how we finally decided.

Sam is lying in the same position with his hands folded behind his head. Ramona is doing a halfway headstand up against the wall. (This is only the second time I have ever seen her without her school uniform. Her jeans are unfashionably baggy and I like that.) She drops sideways suddenly and lands with a thud that rattles the china on the fancy mantelpiece.

"Careful," Sam says. He doesn't even turn his head, and I understood that Ramona making a ruckus in the house is a normal occurrence. He has a small smile too, and I feel like an idiot for not seeing before that he is way, way into her.

I did feel like my brain was functioning better, but we couldn't find a name that we all liked.

"Sam?" Ramona says. She is lying on the floor in her nook now, splayed out like a victim of some violent trauma. "Do you remember when I was describing to you what it felt like when I went glitter bombing with Tom? That's what I wish we could name the band after. That's what making music with you two feels like."

"Yeah," I say.

I know the feeling she was talking about.

Earlier today, before we checked for Nanami's comment, we had band practice. There's a song we started two weeks ago that has never really clicked right. Ramona announced that if we didn't get it together today, we needed to scrap the song, and Sam and I agreed.

We started out the way we had before, with Sam leading on bass. A few bars in, I started the preset counter melody on the kaosolator, and Ramona started a slow military drumming.

I lowered the tone and held it until it turned into a drone.

I remembered the way the blue at the top of the fence blended with the sky (and shined).

And then Sam started a melody on his acoustic guitar.

It was like he'd plucked the blue-on-blue image from my brain and turned it into music.

Ramona slowed time down, and I could see the car drive past the fence and the face of the driver, just a stranger I'll never meet, frowning against his phone. From the corner of my eye, I could still see the blue sparkles in the October light. The sun caught the windshield and sent a glare into my eyes.

And then I was back in the garage, and the song was coming to a close.

"Vandalized by Glitter," I say now. Sam and Ramona both sit up and look at me. "'Vandalized by Glitter' is what the cop said when I got arrested. And I don't know, sometimes our songs sound like we're going up to a person and throwing glitter in their face."

"I hated it until you said the thing about throwing glitter in their face," Sam says. "But now I get it. And I like it."

"Vandalized by Glitter," Ramona says. "*Vandalized*."

"*By Glitter*," I say. I waggle my eyebrows at her. She laughs, and we have a name.

And I have real friends who I think might actually understand me.

♡xΦ Ramona

The band is rocking. Last week we all received our letters from Artibus inviting us to apply to our majors. I'm still in love with Sam, and now I have an inconvenient avalanche of a crush on Tom, although I think I have it under control.

Kind of.

We're two-thirds of the way through the semester.

So of course it's time for me to have a run-in with my nemesis.

All semester, Emmalyn has been on the verge of going too far. It's not that I care what she says about me. It's just that I'm sick of it. I tell myself that she's probably unhappy, maybe jealous. But what right does she have to so actively and publicly dislike me? I've never done anything to her. Unless she did something first.

Like today.

It's dumb, but I'm in a really good mood this morning. It's all starting to seem real now. I would finally be allowed to leave this place. The world would finally start to take seriously my desire to devote my life to music. Also, I'd found a kick-ass pair of black studded leather boots that fall just short of being military boots and therefore just barely pass the school dress code.

So I'm smiling when I walked into class.

A show of genuine emotion to some people.

A sign of weakness to Emmalyn Evans.

"Are those corrective shoes to fix her posture?" she whispers loudly as I sit down. "They aren't working."

I know that my boots are awesome no matter what the Emmalyns of the world say, but I happen to have great fucking posture. I really do.

And that part of her comment pisses me off.

"Good morning, Emmalyn," I say aloud. "It seems that you once again failed to receive enough attention from your father over the weekend."

"Oh God, what is wrong with her?" she asks. And then I snap.

"Talk to me!" I stand up and shout the words at her. "Stop talking about me and. Talk. To. Me."

At that point Dr. Harris has to own up to his sense of hearing, and Emmalyn and I are sent to the office.

Together.

At Saint Joseph's Preparatory, students are expected to have the civility to walk quietly to the office next to their enemy without inflicting injury. As if shivs were more powerful than tongues.

"Oh my God," Emmalyn whispers over and over again. "This is so ridiculous."

"Who are you talking to?" I say. "Are you finally actually talking to me instead of about me?"

"Why am I being sent to the office? I was just talking to Hanna. You were the one screaming at me."

"You were talking about me to the whole room," I say. I have to stop myself before my voice rises again while I'm finally articulating in the heat of the moment what I've been wanting to say to her for years. "Your little guise of just being overheard while indulging in teenage gossip isn't fooling anybody, not even Dr. Harris. You're just a bully."

"I'm not a bully," Emmalyn says. She actually stops in the middle of the hallway and turns to me. "I just don't like you, you or your kind."

"My kind?" I say. This is new. "What the hell do you mean by that?"

"You just have to make sure everybody knows that you are *so* special and *so* weird." She tilts her head higher. "Everything you do, your haircuts and your stupid boots, it's all about proving that you're just so fucking unusual. You say that you don't care what people think, but you do. You probably spend more time on your appearance than I do. You act like you're this tortured and misunderstood outcast, but you're really not, okay? You've got friends, and your hair looks like something from a *Teen Vogue* 'How to Get That Punk Rock Look' column. So get over yourself, Ramona, 'cause we're all sick of hearing about what a unique snowflake you are."

And what she says sounds just right enough that I can't speak. (Am I a poseur?) I just stare at her like an idiot. And then the principal comes out into the hall and reminds us that we're due in his office. And I get the old lecture about the expectations that Saint Joe's has for students, but all I hear is Emmalyn's taunting voice.

We're all tired
     Of hearing about
      What a unique
And special
     Snowflake
You   are.

                   (poseur)
        What if it's true? What if
     I've already been caught by the machine?

Sam

Ramona's dad grounded her after her latest tangle with Emmalyn Evans, so we're not having band practice this week.

I was surprised when Tom called me Thursday afternoon.

I like Tom, but it never occurred to me to hang out with him without Ramona there.

"Do you just wanna get something to eat?" he said. I nodded and then remembered that he couldn't see me do that over the phone.

"Yeah, cool," I said.

We were waiting in the drive-through when it happened; we saw the poster.

"I hate shit like that," Tom said. He pointed at the side of the building where an ad for the fast-food place hung. The picture was supposed to be of a woman eating the new

Snack Big burger they're pushing, but it didn't even look like she was eating.

It looked like she's trying to make out with the sandwich.

"I guess a female having sex with a burger will make males buy it," I said.

"I hate society," Tom said. "I really, really, really do. All of this misogynistic bullshit should have been fixed long before we were even born."

"I guess it falls to us to fix it then." I was talking about society when I said that, but I guess Tom thought I meant the poster.

"Sam, you are so, so right," he said. And then he climbed out of my car, went up to the poster frame, and removed the girl and her burger lover.

"What is happening?" I said as he got back in the car.

"We're gonna fix the poster, like you said," Tom said. "Now just pay for our food and act normal. Do you have art supplies at your house?"

I did not have art supplies.

Grift Craft is in Soulard, a gentrified neighborhood on the edge of the city, and Tom told me not to judge the store too harshly based on that.

"They still have to turn a profit after all," he reasoned as

I parallel parked. I nodded, but inwardly I was laughing that Tom thought I might hold it against him that his favorite craft store is in a yuppie neighborhood.

Outside of the car, Tom stood back and swept his arm dramatically against the skyline of redbrick buildings.

"People have been living in this neighborhood since the late seventeen hundreds, and that is the kind of thing that is always cool." Tom said.

I nodded again, this time in perfect agreement.

The inside of Grift Craft looked like an urban witch's garden. Things were hung from fishing wire from the ceiling and crowd along shelves. "Things" is as specific as I can get. Mirrors caught the light. Metal objects clanged and chimed against each other in the air currents. Art projects perched on every surface, and the walls were covered in frames and shelves. There were a thousand things to look at, and a thousand painted or sketched, plastic or Styrofoam eyes looking back at me.

"Ramona told me about this place," I said.

"Yeah, she loved it," Tom said. The store is an odd shape, and the aisles make it even stranger, but he led me with ease to the stencils at the back of the store.

"So what's our message? I mean, maybe some woman out

there would want to have sex with a hamburger (and that's totally fine), but people need to realize that they are being manipulated. How do we show that, Sam?"

We stood in front of the stencils and he looked at me imploringly. He genuinely wanted to know what I thought, and he was going to stand there staring at me until I told him.

"Most people are actually pretty smart when they remember to actually stop and think about things," I said.

❧

CONSUME
CONSUME
CONSUME
AND DIE WITHOUT THINKING
ABOUT IT

said the poster we placed in the frame outside the restaurant very late on Friday night. Tom insisted that the words be outlined in red glitter. Alongside the words the woman still pressed the burger into her face. We didn't change anything on her image, but now it looked more like she was being smothered by the burger.

The next day we went through the drive-through in the late afternoon, and the employees still hadn't taken it down.

"This is the greatest compliment we could ever receive," Tom said. "No one's told the manager yet. It means they like it. You've taught me a lesson, Sam. I must never forget that most people are actually pretty smart and actually pretty cool."

And I finally understood what Ramona knew all along.

Tom was meant to meet us in same way a meteor is destined to crash into whatever is along its trajectory.

Tom

Here's how Sara broke up with me.

She called me late in the afternoon and said she was coming by. She'd finally saved enough money to buy her own car. She'd quit her job at the mall so that she could do an internship at her dad's company over the summer.

School wasn't even out yet, but I hardly ever saw her anymore.

(And, yeah, it's all obvious to me now.)

So I waited for her out on the front porch, and after she parked, I walked down the steps. I met her on the sidewalk and kissed her cheek. She started crying.

"Tom, just don't," she said. "Don't even try."

"Try what?" I asked. I felt like the baffled boyfriend on a sitcom. She just stood there crying, and I just stood there doing nothing.

"You don't feel that way about me. I know that you don't," she finally said.

"What way?" I said.

"You don't want to have sex with me," Sara said, standing on the sidewalk outside my parents' house. "God, not that I'm ready. But you—you—" There were tears studding her eyelashes. Her ponytail was slipping down, and the setting sun made a halo out of her loosened hair.

She was so beautiful.

She was right.

"You get bored kissing me," Sara said. "You hold me and never try anything else. You know it's true."

"I love you, Sara," I said. I knew that it was true.

"I know you do," she said. "But you're gay, Tom. And that's okay, but—"

"I'm not—"

"We need to break up."

"I'm not gay," I said. I put my hands on her shoulders to steady both of us. "I just don't feel that way about anybody."

There.

I'd said it.

I'd told Sara what I had never said aloud to anyone ever before.

"You don't…" She frowned and shook her head.

"I'm not gay. I'm not straight. I just don't really care about sex."

"You don't care. About sex." She said it like I'd said I didn't care about curing cancer.

"I don't know why," I said. I tried to gather together my years of puzzling over this and lay it all before her. "I just never developed this obsession with sex that everyone else has. It's never interested me, and it just seems to cause everyone else a lot of trouble. But I love you, Sara. I think you're so smart and beautiful, and I love being with you. I just don't want to have sex with you."

I looked at her, and she looked at me, and I hoped that she could accept me.

"No, Tom," she said. "That's not possible."

"It's true. I—"

"You need to do some thinking, Tom," she said. It was starting to annoy me how often she was saying my name. "Everybody's sexual. You're in denial about something, and it's not fair to either of us to keep up with this charade of a relationship."

She turned away from me and got into her car.

And I let her go.

Because to me it had never been a charade,

To me our relationship had been everything I had ever
wanted,
But to her, it had been missing the most basic human need.
There was nothing to do but let her go.
After that I was alone.

Until Ramona found me.

And she introduced me to Sam.

(And I started to think that maybe it was
safe to get close to someone again.)

♡ xo Ramona

It's been a long time since I've been able to play the piano
for fun.

This past week and a half, I've spent every afternoon
alone with the piano in Dad's condo.

Playing without practicing.

I'd forgotten what that felt like.

Bach is my favorite. He is the rock-star king of
baroque music.

I've also been indulging in the Tori and Fiona songs I
used to obsessively play at thirteen.

It feels so good to take the empty condo and fill it with
a song that I love.

I adore this long stand of black and white,

the vibration and rumbles

of this instrument,

the pedals under my feet.

When I was little, this was how I spent most of my time.

It made Dad happy, and I didn't have any close friends back then. Back then, playing the piano felt like my purpose.

Beavers build dams.

Bees make honey.

Ramona plays piano.

My whole world was structured around the piano. It was my joy and my passion, and every adult I knew praised me for my dedication.

And then something changed, in the way that things always change.

I went to junior high at McKinley, a magnet school in the city. All through sixth and seventh grade, I looked with longing at the musicians in eighth grade. If they passed the audition, they got to take advanced music with Mrs. Trundle, my favorite teacher. The advanced music students played in an ensemble, and they were invited to play with the St. Louis Symphony at Powell Hall in the spring, where the best student would also play a solo.

In my early-adolescent mind, playing that spring concert solo was the objective of my being.

In the weeks before the audition, I slaved over the piano, and I wept with joy when I was accepted into the class. On the first day of eighth grade, my leg jiggled nervously under my desk in each class, impatient to reach the goal of the last line on my schedule.

Finally, last period came.

I burst into the music room and found that Mrs. Trundle was not there.

Mr. Jones was there. He had red hair, a bizarre tie that looked like a lightning bolt, and new ideas. He stood in front of the classroom and shattered me to the very core.

"You are here because you are gifted and therefore worthy of being challenged. And that means going out of your comfort zone. The instrument you auditioned with is not the instrument you will be playing with the symphony this spring."

We were told that over the next few months we would all be trying out new instruments, and by the end of the semester, we would select the instrument we would then focus on for the spring concert.

I hated Mr. Jones.

I hated his tie and his words and his face.

I hated him with a fiery passion you cannot imagine.

Just cut to a scene of me sullenly scratching on a violin

in the corner of the music room, my icy eyes focused on Mr. Jones as he joyously instructs a student at the piano.

Then, Friday came.

And we were told that as a special treat we would have a drum circle.

I hated Mr. Jones and his stupid hippie ways.

But the rhythm got to me.

I'd grimly grabbed the bongo without thought, but I found myself fascinated by the varying texture of sound. The drums weren't the simple instrument that I'd thought.

I hated Mr. Jones, but on Monday I went to the corner where he kept the percussion instruments.

In the spring concert, I played the xylophone, a percussion instrument that uses chimes laid out like a keyboard. It was familiar enough that the solo I coveted had gone to me by a landslide. Afterward, I hugged Mr. Jones with tears in my eyes.

And told my dad that I absolutely had to use my birthday money on a drum kit.

I still play piano, but I play the drums too.

Loving the drums hasn't made me love piano less.

Just as Sam has stayed in my heart even after I fell for Tom.

Some things, it seems, are always the same even after things change.

Sam

"That is the coolest thing you have ever done," Ramona said. We were at school on Monday, under the stairwell by the music department, where we first met. I was showing her the pic on my phone of the poster. "I get grounded, and you immediately go off and do the coolest thing ever."

"You went glitter bombing with Tom," I reminded her.

"Yeah." She paused and cocked her head to the side. "When I go off with Tom, we do something subtle and quiet, but Tom and you go do something loud and inyourface."

"I get the feeling that Tom is the sort of guy who brings the hidden side out of a person," I said.

Ramona smiled. "You get it now, don't you? You understand why we needed him in the band."

"Yeah," I said. "I do. I don't know how you knew, but you were right." She smiled again and adjusted her book bag.

"I really like him," she said.

"Yeah, me too."

"I mean—I mean I *like* like him, Sam. Tom."

"Oh," I said. I'm such an idiot.

"Is that cool? I don't want to mess stuff up with the band." She shrugged her shoulders and averted her eyes, then glanced up at me from under her eyelashes. So pretty.

Damn her for being so pretty.

"Of course it's cool," I said. "I want you to date whoever you want."

I want you to want to date me, I didn't say.

Ramona got this soft, sad look on her face.

"You're such a good friend to me," she said.

The warning bell rang, reminding us that we were supposed to be headed to class.

"I'll see you after school for band practice!" she yelled, and turned and ran up the stairs, away from me.

Away from

me.

Tom

I'm hanging out with Ramona at her place today. She and her dad live in a condo in the city. It's nice, but it's not anything like Sam's mom's brownstone, which has four stories and the kind of sprawling lawn one rarely sees in metropolitan areas.

Ramona's front door has a tiny patch of grass with a green giggling Buddha sitting by the door. The inside is crowded with the grand piano and her father's bookshelves. It's obvious that they are a family focused on intellectual pursuits.

We're in her bedroom now. Her dad reminded her to leave the door open. She has a posters of Chopin, Björk, Kathleen Hanna, and Evelyn Glennie on her walls. Her bedspread is pink and girlie. I didn't expect that.

"For elementary school, I went to this hippie charter where we had this class called 'Art with Found Materials,'" Ramona is saying. "We literally went to junkyards and made stuff. And yesterday"—she holds up a large tin can with a long spring attached that dances just above the floor—"I remembered the day I made one of these." She finishes with a flourish and shakes the can.

The spring sways and thrums, echoing inside the can. It sounds like a thunderous, ominous wind filling the room. It sounds like the wind inside my car, the noise I've been trying and failing to replicate electronically.

(Ramona is probably the coolest girl I know.

And I don't know why I said "probably."

She just is. The Coolest.)

"I also know how to make a tambourine out of bottle caps," she says. She sits down on the carpet next to me.
(She reminds me of Sara,

but at the same time,

I've never met anyone like her.)

"We should do a piece where you and Sam play home-made instruments, and I record you guys and play it back with weird effects," I say.

"Yes!" Ramona shouts. She flings her arms wide and the spring rattles.

I laugh.

"What?" she says.

"You," I say. I'm smiling, and so is she.

But I'm still unprepared when she leans forward to kiss me.

Maybe I should have been expecting it, but I'm just not good at these things.

So I have to make a decision fast.

I think I might like to be with her like that,

(kind of)

and she *is* the coolest girl I know.

So we kiss.

I like it.

But after a while it's just

A little boring.

A little wet.

And afterward we hold hands, which I like, and we talk about going to the art museum with Sam, which sounds fun.

And Ramona smiles this secret smile now, reveling in this thing I only kind of understand.

♡xoRamona

Tom.

Tom.

Tom. Tom. Tom.

Tom.

TOM.

I kissed Tom.

Then we smiled, and we talked and we laughed, and before he left for home, he kissed me good night and told me he'd call me.

It's all so natural.

So right.

TOM.

Tom. Tom.

I can't believe I actually did it.

I leaned forward and I kissed him like I was this cool, confident chick.

I was worried that he would think my kissing was awkward.

I hadn't actually kissed someone since eighth grade.

And a guy like Tom who is so cool, he's got to be experienced.

But he kissed me back. He likes me too.

Tomorrow after school we'll go to Sam's garage and make music together.

We'll hold hands and laugh.

We'll be boyfriendandgirlfriend and all will be well.

(And I'll forget to ache when I look at Sam.)

Sam

I knew this day would come, so it was easy to pretend that I didn't mind. I knew that someday, someone would see Ramona the way I do.

I knew there would be someone who she wanted too.

I'm not saying that this doesn't hurt like hell.

Because it does hurt like hell.

It hurts like hell.

There we were, sitting on the floor of my garage as if it were an ordinary Thursday, listening to the final mix on our best song. It's the most professional-sounding thing we've ever done.

Tom sat cross-legged and lamented our earlier and loooonger winter break. We'll be off three days before him, but we go back to school only two days before him.

Ramona had her hand on his knee.

And it's amazing how this simple fact changed everything.

Her hand was so still.

Still in a way that Ramona never is, never is with me.

Her fingers draped over his kneecap and rested on the denim of his jeans.

At school today she said, "Tom and I are together now."

And I said, "Cool," as if it was, and then we talked about other things. Apparently Emmalyn has been ignoring Ramona, which she thinks is grand. But this was all I could think about: how later I would be sitting here. Sitting here with them.

Ramona's fingers had chipped nail polish on them.

She never paints her nails. She must have done it last night (for him), but of course the polish was already chipped.

I thought about her hand on my knee—a soft, quiet weight telling me that she's mine. Now that I could see her with Tom, the picture was there in my mind, with me in his place.

"Guys, this song is amazing," she said to us. Her fingertips pressed into his knee, not mine. "We're a real band now. Not just kids fooling around in a garage."

I guess that's how she thought of us before Tom.

April and the Rain.

Just kids.

In a garage.

And maybe the band is much better now.

And maybe I really like Tom.

But right now I wish we'd never met him.

Tom

Another girl who wants something from me that I don't know how to give.

Another friend I'm terrified to lose.

Another girlfriend.

But maybe this time it'll be different.

Maybe I'll be different.

Maybe this time I'll feel what everyone else seems to know how to feel.

Maybe this time I won't screw everything up.

And maybe Sam won't hate me for "stealing" Ramona.

'Cause that's another thing I have to worry about.

This is why sex seems like a big waste of energy to me.

The afternoon before Thanksgiving, we drive to Soulard together in my car, with Sam in the backseat. I've got the handheld recorder that has allowed me to capture every-thing from rain on the porch roof to my mother cooking bacon. We're planning on walking around and asking dif-ferent people what they're thankful for and recording their answers. I'm gonna run some effects on the voices, and Ramona and Sam are gonna make the music to play under it.

We park at Grift Craft because I know Teddy won't mind. Teddy is the owner. As soon as I learned to drive, I became such a regular customer that Teddy and I got to talking. And talking led to long discussions about music and art, and now he gives me work on the weekends for cash under the table. I haven't mentioned that I have a job to Ramona or Sam yet because I already feel so outclassed by them.

(I know that's dumb, and they aren't snobby types at all, but emotions aren't logical, okay? Plus, they might disap-prove of me stocking yarn on the black market.)

It's a gorgeous autumn day, crisp and bright. The gold leaves glow against the redbrick buildings. College students back home and mingling with their high school friends are parking their cars and walking to the bars that fill the gentri-fied neighborhood.

They are ripe pickings for our picking. Recording. (Whatever.)

We do a few test takes to make sure the recorder is working, and then I jump in front of the first twentysomething I see.

"What are you thankful for?" I shout at her. She jumps back, startled, and blinks at me.

"My dog," she says. Her friend laughs at her and tugs on her arm, dragging her away from the crazy kids with a microphone in the street. I pass the mic to Sam.

"Do you have anything to be thankful for?" Ramona asks a passing man. He's older—thirtyish. Sam readies the mic under his chin. He scowls at us.

"Privacy," he barks. This time Ramona laughs, and the sound registers on the recorder. She has such a pretty laugh.

She grins at me and tucks some hair behind her ear.

I appreciate how pretty she is, like a rambunctious sunset.

I should feel something more than I do.

I smile back at her.

Sam isn't looking at us; he's holding the recorder out in front of a group of bleached blonds.

"What are you thankful for?"

"My friends," one shouts.

"Me too," I say. I smile at Ramona and look over my shoulder at Sam. He glances at us and looks away. But he doesn't look angry. He passes the recorder to Ramona again.

She dashes off in the direction of an old woman walking an ancient poodle.

"Hey, man," I say. I can't look at him, and I realize I haven't figured out exactly what I want to say. "I don't want to take her away."

"No…" he mumbles. Ramona grins in reply to the old woman and turns to run back to us. "We're cool, dude."

We haven't met eyes. We watch Ramona race back to us, her smile beaming at us both.

I can do this.

I can balance this.

I can still have this.

♡✗Ramona

"So, you're *dating* this Tom now?" Dad says.

"This Tom?" I say. "He's *this* Tom now?" We're in the kitchen. I'm spooning jambalaya out of the Crock-Pot. Pretty much all of Dad's cooking is Crock-Pot based. For most of my life, I had no idea that this was weird, but now I think it's weird that it's weird, because everybody should cook with a Crock-Pot. It's so convenient and you can make almost anything.

Anyway.

"Yes, Moany," Dad says. "He's *this* Tom for now, but he'll become *that* Tom if I see any trouble with him." I roll my eyes and sit down on the other stool at the kitchen island, across from him.

And yeah. Dad's name for me is Moany. Or sometimes Moany-Moans. When he's teasing me for being whiny, he calls me "Her Moaniness." That one really drives me crazy.

"He's nice, Daddy," I say. "You'll like him." Overall Dad

really is cool. And he's a good cook. Don't let the Crock-Pot thing throw you.

"Does Sam like him?"

"Of course Sam likes him!" I say. "Do you think that I could like a guy who Sam didn't like?"

"It's a common enough trope in modern storytelling. Almost as common as the platonic friends who are secretly in love."

Really, I can't roll my eyes enough at the man. I mean, he always talks like he's on NPR, and he also thinks that he's subtle.

"Sam and I are just friends," I tell him for the forty-millionth time, because it is technically, my own feelings aside, true. "Tom is my boyfriend now, and he's nice and smart and unique. And we've started a new band with him. We're Vandalized by Glitter now. We have this fuller, strange, new sound now."

"Well," Dad says, "I'm sure he's decent enough if you like him, but bring him around again soon, okay? I want to get to know *this* Tom sooner rather than later. And make sure that he doesn't cut into your piano practice. Your mother went on her first tour when she was twenty-one, remember."

"I know," I say. "I practiced for two hours yesterday, and I can do three hours tomorrow."

"And don't forget that you have finals at the end of the month. School is just as important as piano."

"I know."

"You're a talented pianist, Ramona. I just want you to live your full potential."

"I know, Daddy," I say.

But I'm a talented drummer too, Daddy, I do not say.

Sam

When I'm with Ramona, it's not that bad.

She's so happy that it's making her extra goofy, and I'm spending so much time laughing that I sort of forget why she's so happy. When I pick her up for school, she's awake and giggling and telling me about something she saw on the Internet the night before. At school Emmalyn has done at least one terrible thing to report on, and on the way to my place for band practice, Ramona is bursting with ideas and observations for Vandalized by Glitter. I want her, but it's always been that way.

When I'm with Ramona and Tom it's worse, but it's not that bad.

They act almost the same, and they only kiss good-bye, so I can always try and miss it.

It's when I'm alone,

(And it's always dark by then.)

It's when I'm alone that it's bad.

And I think about how much I want to be with her. How much I want to touch her and kiss her. How much I just want to sit with her and say in an ordinary way, "I love you, Ramona."

Ramona.

Ramona is with Tom.

I can't hate Tom. Tom's a cool guy. Tom's my friend.

Ramona's a pretty girl; of course Tom would like her.

It's just that I want to be with her. I want to be the one, the one that gets to have her love, the one who gets to touch her face. I want to be the one she wants to have with her. The one she calls her one.

But he's not me.

Tom

I love making things. I love taking paper and paint and creating an image that had only been in my mind but that now I can show people and try to explain. It's my way of talking about my feelings.

I love music. I feel it in my chest and in my hands and in my feet. Music is more than just something I hear; it's something that happens to me. I can communicate better with music than with words.

I love my parents and my brothers. Even though they don't get me (they really don't), they still love me. I know that I'm lucky to have a family, and I love them.

And I love Sam and Ramona. We haven't been friends all that long, but I feel like we were always meant to meet. I love the way Sam never speaks unless he's thought for some time about what he's going to say, so that he can say it just right. I love the way that Ramona is so alive and full of thoughts and emotions that the words just can't wait to get out of her mouth.

I love talking with them about music and art and the world. I love making music with them. I love it that they're starting to make art with me.

I have a lot of love in my life. I don't feel like I'm missing out on anything.

I don't know why I don't feel sexual urges, but I don't.

I didn't have anything horrible happen to me as a child.

I've told a doctor and been checked out. Nothing's wrong with me.

Except that something must be wrong, right?

Right?

So I should try to be with Ramona in the way she wants. I should try to feel sexual desire. Maybe it's like a muscle that can be exercised. Maybe I can be jump-started, and then I'll still be me, but I'll have this thing that everyone else feels.

♡x℗Ramona

Similar to eighth grade, my last class of the day, my advanced orchestra class, would be the best part of my school day if it wasn't for the presence of one person.

But if you think I'll be hugging Emmalyn at the end of this year, overwhelmed by the life lesson I just learned, then, . well, this story is not for you.

Emmalyn plays the violin. She's actually kinda good.

But that's not the point. No one said I hated her because she was a bad musician.

At Saint Joe's, advanced orchestra is basically just a study hall for music. People sit in corners and run scales, practice pieces for upcoming evaluations, that kind of thing. Normally, Emmalyn and I don't interact much here, though I can still hear her obnoxious laugh from time to time, and I swear she does it on purpose every time I walk by.

And today she stole my metronome.

It's the school's metronome, but I was using it. I got up

to go to the bathroom, and when I came back, it was not on the piano anymore. Emmalyn was practicing with it on the other side of the music room. So the only thing to do was to march over there and demand it back from her.

"What do you mean, your metronome?" she said in the high pitch her voice gets when she's being snotty. "It's the school's metronome, and we're supposed to be sharing it. There are sixteen of us and four metronomes, and you've snagged one every single day all semester. That math says you're hogging them."

"What are you talking about? Math?" My voice was probably starting to rise too, because I saw a few people glancing over. "I was using that metronome, plain and simple. And you can't just take it from me." I reached toward the metronome on the table next to her. Emmalyn squawked and swatted my hand with her bow. It didn't hurt, but instinctively I pulled my hand back.

"You are unbelievable. You're like a five-year-old! Didn't your mother teach you to share?" I said.

"My mother is dead, you bitch," she said.

And I was so surprised,

that I said,

"Mine too."

We stared at each other, and then thankfully the bell rang.

And I'm taking a metronome tomorrow. John has been pushing me hard on the scales, and Dad is counting on me. Emmalyn isn't going to get in my way.

(Even if her mother is dead.)

Sam

"Last night when I came in the garage, it looked like Ramona and Tom were holding hands," Mom said. We were eating Korean takeout, and then we would have the crème brûlée Mom made for dessert.

"Yeah, they're doing that now," I said. "It's not a big deal."

"They're going out?" she asked.

"Yup," I said. "But it's not a big deal, Mom."

"You're okay with that?"

"Yeah. I mean, I kinda have to be. But it's not a big deal."

"Tell me if you need to talk," she said. I focused on finishing my food after that. The moment I was done, Mom started putting the leftovers away. She's big on eating leftovers and only cooking when it's fun.

She used to say "Tell me if you need to talk" a lot after the divorce. I couldn't really take her up on it though. She was too much of a mess for me to add to her burden.

So I talked to Ramona instead when I needed to talk to someone.

Mom pulled out the little blowtorch she bought for melting sugar. She fiddled with the knob and tapped it on the table.

"Now how does this work?" she mumbled.

Once a month my dad picks me up on a Saturday afternoon. We go to a Cardinals game or to see a new exhibit at the art museum. Then we go to a late dinner at an expensive steak house. Dad asks me questions about school. He asks my opinions on current events. That night I sleep in the guest bedroom of his downtown loft.

In the morning he drives me home. Even after he bought me my car, our routine never varied. He could see me more if he wanted to. He never calls me. He trusts that the money he spends will keep me safe for the next month.

When he lived with us, he was hardly ever around, and he'd been satisfied with third-person updates. Now I actually have a period of focused attention.

I used to be angrier about it.

But talking to Ramona made me realize that being angry was pointless.

All it did was hurt me, without any effect on the situation.

So I'm not angry with Tom for being with Ramona.

Tom and Ramona care about each other; that's a good thing.

But I still don't have anyone to talk to about it.

"I'm not angry at Tom," I said. I watched my mother as she delicately ran the flame across the sugar snow. "But I guess I do wish I were in his place."

And my mom, she didn't overdo it.

"That must suck," she said as she flicked off the torch. "Does Ramona know how you feel?"

Tom

So.

There was just too much shit going on, and I fucking had to make some art.

It's almost Christmas, and all around us, people are equating material goods with love. (Some of these commercials scare me.)

So I thought I'd make a statement about first-world materialism in the face of world hunger, 'cause you know, it's Christmas.

I'd make a poster for the mall parking garage. Something to shock people into knowing what I know—that some people are starving and other people are buying stupid stuff.

I'd find the saddest image I could and put something under it like "Ask her what she wants for Christmas."

So I searched for "starving child" images.

(Do not search for "starving child.")

And I learned that I knew nothing.

I did not know that an infant could be stretched so thin
that it would scare me.

I did not know. I did not know.

That babies have skulls and ribs and eyes that can scream.
I did not know
We all are skeletons,
Corpses walking around with life-flesh encasing us for now.
And all it takes is the tip of a scale, and you're just living
bones and
paper skin.
Ready to be forgotten.
If it weren't for journalists with cameras and teenagers with
something to prove.

So.

I didn't do the project.

Because my problems are that I have a girlfriend and
a best friend, my parents want to talk to me while we eat
dinner together (which we do every night), and I think going
to school takes up too much of my time.

I took some money out of my savings account and

donated it to a world hunger charity. And I went downstairs and looked at our Christmas tree.

I sat there for a long, long time.

♡x°Ramona

The morning after Christmas, I lay in bed for a long time. The light had that winter feeling of thick, cold cloud cover. My bedroom overlooks the alley and the neighbor's brick wall.

No grass, no trees, just the red brick and dirty mortar, one iron star support, and a small triangle of sky.

I love my window's wall. I've watched late-afternoon light drift across it in sadness and in joy, and I've stared toward it at night and wondered, *What is life for?*

I know a special crack in a certain brick.

I think I could fit the top of my thumb in one chipped corner, but I suppose I'll never know for sure, since it's up at the third floor.

What I'm trying to say is that you could take a picture of this wall and a bunch of other redbrick walls, and I could pick mine out. Easily.

What I'm trying to say is that I love this brick wall because it's the brick wall that's been outside my window all my life.

But it could have been another brick wall in another place. Or a hedge. Or a bridge.

The morning after Christmas, I lay in bed and watched my wall and I thought, *Sometimes love is like that.* It's about a certain time and place, circumstances that could have changed. Tom says he doesn't think his parents would like him if he were someone else's son, but he is theirs and they love him, so it's fine. There were friends I had in junior high because we were there at the same time, and when we weren't there, we weren't friends anymore, and that was fine.

People you don't know blend together as identical as Pink Floyd's bricks in a wall.

But when I met Tom, it was like he was already my wall.

Okay.

Wait.

It was like when I've had a bad day. And I'm tired. And I finally go into my room at the end of the day and I see the window, and I remember that I've felt this bad before, but it always gets better again, that life happens in cycles.

When I met Tom, that's how it felt. Like Tom's very existence in the world reminded me that I was Ramona, drummer and pianist, and I was gonna get into Artibus, get out of high school, and get on with my life as a musician. A musician.

And he reminds me of this every time I see him.

I am in love. With Tom. And with Sam, who I knew was my Sam as soon as I met him.

Some people don't think this could be true.

But I do.

I am.

I love.

Sam

Ramona has to practice piano a lot during school breaks, so Tom and I have been hanging out without her. He never talks about Ramona in a way that makes me uncomfortable. You'd never know they were going out except when she's in the room.

It's easy to pretend it's not true.

Tom loves the series of guitar and guitar-like instruments that my father buys each Christmas and birthday. Yesterday he played the sitar and I played the banjo, and we made up a song called "Hamlet." The lyrics are "Words, words, words."

Tuesday, we glitter bombed a slide in the park. Now it has the words *FREE TO BE HAPPY* written in yellow, glittery puff paint down its blue plastic side. Three days and it's still there; it's kinda endearing how happy that makes Tom.

Today, we hung out at his place. Tom's room is really small, but he's covered every inch of the walls with images and words, some big, some small. It's kind of oppressive but still awesome. We were talking about Ramona's drumming, and he said, "She's really just a pure percussionist. It's no surprise that her second instrument is the piano."

"It's her first instrument actually," I said.

"Well, she started playing it first, but Griselda is her main instrument now," he said.

"Nope," I said. "Ask her about it. She'll tell you that piano is her main instrument." I was standing, wandering around the room, studying the walls. "Art Is the Proper Task of Life" said a bumper sticker near me.

"But her heart is with her drum kit," he said. He was sitting on the floor, leaning against the bed.

"Yeah, I know. But it's with the piano too, 'cause of her mom. You know."

"Oh," he said. But it didn't sound like he knew. I got the feeling that she hadn't said much to him about her mom, and I couldn't help but be happy about that.

"What's this?" I asked. I touched a photograph that hadn't been there before. I thought it was something from a horror movie at first glance, but I realized it's a baby, skeleton thin and large eyed.

Behind me, I heard the floorboards creak as Tom shifted.

"I put it there to remind myself that I'm lucky to have more than I need."

He sounded embarrassed, so I let it drop.

"Let's make some music," I said.

And we did. And it was great. Because Ramona was right. Tom is a great musician, and we were meant to meet him and be his friend, and they were meant to be together.

It's true.

Even though I wish that I was meant to be with Ramona too.

(Too?)

Tom

"You have to participate in the senior showcase," Ally Tabor says to me the first day back at school. She's linked arms with me in the hallway as if we're the very bestest of friends who always walk together.

"Hi, Ally. My break was great. Thanks for asking," I say. (It's funny that she's accosted me today. I've been thinking about the two-and-a-half-week romance we shared, what with Ramona and all. Mom was making me participate in at least one club that semester because I "needed to make friends." I went to the drama club meetings, and for a little while Ally wanted to hold my hand, and then she didn't. The next semester Mom didn't make me have a club.)

"Please, Tom! Please. If we don't have enough interest this year, then they may not have a senior showcase next year." Her eyes widen at this terrible possibility.

"And since we won't be here next year…" I say.

"Tom, the senior showcase is about more than just

our senior year. It's about all the seniors that have ever—"
Then she prattles on about traditions and passing torches.
Like I said before, Ally takes her drama club presidency
very seriously.

"Just do one of your music-like things, Tom," she says as
she deposits me outside my next class.

"Music-like things?" I say. I roll my eyes.

"You're going to end up participating. You just wait,"
Ally says. "You're secretly dying to show our classmates your
music, and I have a long-term plan for wearing you down.
Bye!" She scurries off to class or to conquer a small nation.

And I am not participating.

♡x♡Ramona

Sam and I haven't been alone in a while.

Except, we have been alone. We're alone in his car on the way to and from school, but it's not a long enough drive for a deep conversation. And at school we sit alone (together) when we eat, but during lunch you can't get really deep because people are throwing fries at each other.

After school Sam and I are always with Tom. And I love being with Tom, but I miss being with just Sam.

On Monday I said to Sam at band practice, "We should go see that martial arts movie you were talking about," even though I knew that I wasn't going to like it. We were talking about theaters and times when from across the garage Tom shouted, "We should just go on Friday," and I was so annoyed for two reasons.

Tom didn't even know what movie we were talking about. Sam had only just told me about it that morning, and this was just supposed to be a me-and-him thing. Furthermore,

I'd been hoping that Tom and I could go on an actu-al date on Friday. We're with Sam all the time, and I really love being with Sam, but I'd kinda like to make out with Tom.

Not that I don't also want to make out with Sam, but that's a totally different problem, and the thing is I *can* make out with Tom, except that I can't because of Sam.

Anyway.

I was really annoyed about all this, so I said, "Fine." And I stalked over to my drums and started playing the drums part of "My Generation" really loud. Sam and Tom looked at each other and I got angrier. Eventually they joined in with me, but then Tom started changing up the melody, and then we all started going crazy with it and it got fun, and I forgot about being mad. For a while.

Sam

On Friday we all went to the Delmar Loop and saw the kung fu movie I'd told Ramona about. It was amazing. People who make fun of martial arts movies just haven't seen the right one yet.

This was the case with Tom.

"Dude. Dude," he said as we exited the theater. "Dude, I had no idea. I'd always written off martial arts as, well, not art." It was dark out. The streets were crowded with people walking to and from ethnic restaurants and boutique stores. Tom kept stride with me; Ramona was walking a bit behind us. I could tell she hadn't liked the movie. She was quiet too, and not telling us why she didn't like it.

"I'm not an aggressive guy, you know?" Tom continued. "Martial arts movies never interested me because I'm not interested in fighting. But for most of human history, fighting was a regular part of life. And somewhere along the way, some people made it art. They added these human values of technique and honor."

Up ahead, a group of transient kids sat in a row, leaning against the vintage record store. One of them strummed a guitar with a case open in front of him. Out of the corner of my eye, I saw Ramona reach into her jeans pocket. Her face was uncharacteristically unexpressive, un-Ramona.

"That movie was about respect and self-discipline," Tom said. We stopped in front of the guitar case. Beside the guy with the guitar was a dreadlocked girl. One of her hands was in a mitten, and it rested on that guy's knee. As we'd approached, I'd seen them share a smile. On the other side of her, another guy was resting his head on her shoulder. She was holding his hand too, and he was wearing the other mitten. They all looked a little older than twenty-one and had that gutter-punk smell of BO and pot. Tom and Ramona threw change into the guitar case. I didn't think the guy was much good, so I didn't feel obligated.

"I'm gonna have to rethink my personal definition of art now," Tom said as we walked away. "I love doing that." Behind me I heard Ramona laugh a strange, quiet laugh.

"We should get coffee Sunday morning," I said. Tom

never wakes up in the morning if he doesn't have to. He never even considers the option.

"Yeah," Ramona said. "That sounds great."

"God, I wanna do that," Tom said.

"What?" I said.

"I want to do what those guys are doing." He motioned over his shoulder to the gutter punks. "I want to live out of a backpack for a few years, only own the necessities of living. And just live."

And then he went off on one of his ideological rants, the sort that normally leaves me inspired. But all I could think about was Ramona. And how she was walking so quietly.

Tom

I feel as if all the years of my life I have been
slowly filling up with a force of nature.
I feel as if my muscles have slowly been tightening,
readying to pounce.
All the places I've never been.
All of the art I want to make.
All of the changes I hunger to see.
And all around me voices are telling me to wait, wait.
Wait.
But inside of me I hear, "Ready, set—"
I want to run.
I want to drive across America.
I want to write.
I want to make music like no one has ever heard.
I'm ready. Let me go.
Because I'm afraid if I don't leave soon,
the voices around me will grow hands

that push and pull.

And as I raise my foot to take my first step,

the ground before me will turn into a path.

A path with a maze of walls,

a destination I cannot escape,

a destiny I never desired.

Why can no one believe in my fear?

The safe and sane life terrifies me.

I need freedom.

I need chance, happenstance.

I need to live a life of learning,

a life that never reaches a final destination.

I want to work.

I want to make the world a better place.

But I don't want to do it by living the way most people choose.

I want the choice to choose

My Living.

My Life.

♡x♡Ramona

Sam and I go to what I think of as "our coffee shop." It's in one of those rough neighborhoods where people are buying up old houses and making them trendy and cute, but sometimes if you're lucky, you'll still come across people having inappropriate arguments in the street.

The suburbs never have good people watching.

Anyway.

Our coffee shop always has art from some local artist on display. Usually it's at least pretty okay, but today it's awful. It's the sort of photography where you suspect the guy was like, "Black and white makes it artsy!"

"Okay," I say as we sit down at a tiny café table. I point to the photo next to us, depicting a girl our age posing by some train tracks. "That was totally taken as a senior portrait."

"Probably. This is some pretty mediocre stuff," Sam agrees.

I've missed you, I think.

"We haven't hung out in a while. Without—"

"Yeah," he says.

The guy behind the counter says, "Peterson!" and Sam gets up to grab our coffees. I watch his backside, thinking that I could always recognize him from behind.

"So," I say when he sits back down. "What's been up with you?"

Sam shrugs his one-shoulder Sam shrug.

"Nothing you don't already know about."

"Right." My heart sinks. I grab four packets of raw sugar, pour them into my cup, and stir until a whirlpool forms strong enough to pull the liquid down deeply toward the middle even after I lift my spoon.

We sip our coffees. My gaze wanders around the coffee shop. It's never like this with us. Normally I can tell Sam anything.

"And you're…good?" he asks. He's looking down at the table, stirring the sugar I spilled around and around.

(His long, dark eyelashes.)

"Yeah," I say. "I'm good."

"And you and Tom are…"

"Good," I say automatically. "Good. I mean—" I take too big a swallow and burn my tongue. I feel myself hold back a grimace. "Sometimes," I say. I look up at Sam.

He looks concerned and interested and gorgeous.

(His eyelashes.)

I look back down at the table.

"Sometimes I wonder if he really wants to be with me," I finally say.

Sam

Ramona, hyperactive and sweet. Jiggling her leg nervously under the table, worrying that someone wouldn't want to be with her.

"Of course he wants to be with you," I said. He's crazy about her. He's always laughing at the things she says. He talks all the time about what a great musician she is, how cool she is.

"It's just, he—" She shrugged and swept the sugar off the table. "I can't explain it. But he doesn't seem that excited about. Being with me."

Ramona, unable to explain something for the first time in her life.

Ramona, too wonderful to be able to comprehend how wonderful she is.

"Some guys are just shy about these things," I told her. "Some guys don't want to seem pushy."

She nodded and shrugged at the same time. Ramona was always Ramona.

"You and Tom aren't exactly alpha males," she said. The corners of her mouth turned up. "That's why I like you both so much."

My heart was beating so hard. I knew this didn't mean anything.

"Just be. You know. Yourself. And Tom will get there," I said and nodded, as if I've given her real advice.

"Yeah," she said. "You're right. Thanks."

I didn't apply to Artibus. I didn't apply.

I don't want to go there. I don't want to major in music. I don't want to struggle to have a career in music. I don't need an exciting life, and I'm not sure if I'd want one. I'd like to travel, but not because I'm on tour. I want to be able to buy a nice enough house and have more than two kids. Maybe as many as four kids.

I want to make music, but I want to make it because I want to, not because I have to. And sometimes, some days, it would be something I didn't want to do. And that's only if I was one of the lucky few who get to have a career.

Ramona breathes music. Being a professional musician will be like being paid to be Ramona.

And she'll make it. She has the talent, and she has the drive.

I only have some talent, and I just don't have the drive.

I know myself.

I didn't apply to Artibus. And I can't tell Ramona.

⚝

"I'm really glad we did this," she said to me as we stood up and carried our empty coffee mugs back to the counter. "I can talk to you about anything."

♡×♡Ramona

It's Valentine's Day, and some girls had flowers that they carried proudly from class to class. I carried in secret the expectation of Tom.

Emmalyn had balloons. Six big, red, rubbery-sounding ones and a giant Mylar one that loves anyone literate. Emmalyn's boyfriend is captain of the debate team and class vice president. He's the sort of boy who poses nobly during gym class. He does big, showy displays of affection for Emmalyn, but he never seems to pay any real attention to her. In the hallways, it seems like he kind of ignores her most of the time. It would make me feel bad for her if I cared.

Anyway.

Ten minutes before school got out, I went over to where Emmalyn was practicing and asked her if she wanted to use the metronome, because I was done using it. She nodded, so I set it down and walked away.

I only did it because I was tired of running scales and ignoring the aching in my fingers. My hands have been cramping lately from practicing so much. John has been pushing me again, telling me that if I want to go pro, I have to work even harder now.

"Your mother would be so proud of you," Dad said to me last night. He doesn't talk about her very often, so I knew that he meant it.

I remember playing piano with my mother. She started teaching me when I was four. I can barely remember those early lessons. Since she died when I was nine, I only saw two sides of her, her mother side and her pianist side. I never got to hear her talk about politics or current events. I know what music she loved, but I don't know what grown-up movies or books she would have shown me. It's hard for me to predict how she would have felt about things.

I'm not sure if she'd approve of what Tom and I are about to do, for one thing. I'm certain that my dad wouldn't, so the odds aren't good.

We're bombing St. Louis with love today.

Tom and I walk down the sidewalk holding hands, just a young couple in love carrying a brown paper grocery bag. While at a nondescript street corner, Tom needs to stop and tie his shoe. He sets down the paper bag and fumbles with his laces. While he's tying his left shoe and then retying his right, I bend down and reach into the bag for just a moment, then roll the top closed again. Tom finishes tying this shoes. He picks the bag back up, and we walk on.

꒰꒱

"Here's your valentine," Tom said to me as he handed me the brown paper bag at my house. I looked at the bag and then back up at him. I knew there had to be something here, but I really didn't get it yet. "Look at the bottom," he added, and then I saw it. The bag was a stencil.

"Sorry I haven't colored it in yet," Tom said. "You're going to have to do that yourself." He opened the bag and put a can of pink spray paint inside.

꒰꒱

We're just a young couple in love walking down the street together. Behind us,

LOVE IS
ALL
YOU NEED

is drying on the sidewalk.

Sam

It's the late February thaw. Today the sun was warm and the gutters were full of melting, dirty snow.

"Okay, okay, okaaaay," Ramona said. "Maybe before we can come up with a definitive definition of 'good music' we need to come up with an ironclad declaration of what 'bad music' is."

She and I were lying on the hood of Tom's glittermobile, just after noon. We drove to the parking lot of an abandoned church building not too far from Ramona's condo, and now we were soaking up vitamin D and talking about music. Tom was doing what he called "some gentle, grounded yoga stretches" on the roof of the car. I recognized lotus and downward dog from Mom's yoga days.

"Bad music is…" Tom started. He breathed out slowly. "Bad music is insincere."

"Bad music *is* insincere," Ramona repeated.

"I've seen sincere musicians who are really terrible," I said. I was thinking of my mother's band, the Whatevers. Mom sang vocals for the Whatevers, but after two shows, she discovered reflexology and the band sort of petered out. At the show I attended, they sang an alt country song called "Catfight." I don't even want to describe it, but Mom was having fun, and the band really liked playing their terrible song.

"Insincere music is bad music," Ramona said, "but not all bad music is insincere music."

"Now we're getting somewhere," Tom said. I couldn't tell if he was being sarcastic. He lay down in corpse pose on the roof. The sun was baking the car nicely, and my body was remembering what summer feels like. I closed my eyes.

"Bad music doesn't make you *feel*," Ramona said.

"Good music always makes you feel," Tom said, "but bad music can make a person feel something too. Haven't you ever seen a carful of people singing along to a generic pop song? And everybody has their secret song."

"Secret song?" Ramona and I said together. I opened my eyes and we glanced at each other as we chuckled.

"Yes!" Tom said. Suddenly his head was peering down above us. He'd flipped onto his stomach. "That song you are too embarrassed to admit that you love! It goes against everything you stand for as a musician, but you can't stand to not dance to it!"

"Ooooh," Ramona said. She reached up and poked his nose with her index finger. He pretended to bite it and she laughed. I closed my eyes again.

"You mean the songs you don't want to come up on random when your friends are with you," Ramona said. "I don't know if dancing is required for that. And I don't believe that you only have one secret song, Tom. I have at least three. Four? It might be four in the summertime. Yeah, four in the summer. And you've convinced me that 'Owner of a Lonely Heart' should be a secret song. Gosh, that's five."

"I am only ashamed of one song," Tom said. "But my shame is so deep that I am never going to admit it."

As soon as he said that, I knew Ramona would never be able to go on with her life until she knew Tom's secret song. I knew that I would be listening to them laugh and argue for the rest of the afternoon. So I kept my eyes closed. I listened to them, and I was able to laugh too.

"Just tell me one thing about your secret song," Ramona moaned.

"You already know that it's a pop song from 1978 that makes me feel inspired," Tom said. "And I know nothing about your ten songs."

"It's only four! I mean five!"

When Ramona asked me, I told her that my secret songs were Meat Loaf's "I'd Do Anything for Love" and "Just Like Heaven" by the Cure.

"The Cure is amazing, man! That is not a secret song!" Tom cried as Ramona laughed and laughed, and gasped, "Meat Loaf!" over and over.

When Ramona laughed, it shook the hood under us. All afternoon, my brain recorded (cherished) each of her subtle movements next to me. With my eyes closed, I didn't have to see her look at Tom, but I could talk with them both and love the sound of her breathing. I heard them kiss once, though Ramona stayed next to me on the hood. He must have bent down, and as Ramona shifted, her thigh pressed against mine for a long moment. My body took in this contact like it was starving for her. With my eyes still closed, I imagined that it was me who had stopped her breathing.

I felt the sun move behind the trees. I knew that if I opened my eyes, there would be glare off the glitter. Ramona admitted to singing along to "I Got You Babe" in the summertime, and Tom revealed that the backup vocals in his secret song were provided by members of Chicago. Their voices got quieter as the sun got dimmer, and the affection in her voice got easier to hear.

And I recognized her tone.

That's Ramona's tone when she's explaining stuff about the kids at school to me, like why everybody thought it was so, so sad that Craig's dad bought him a sedan after he wrecked his convertible.

That's how Ramona talks to me when I'm dropping her off just before her curfew, and I have the engine running, but for some reason she just keeps laughing at all the things I say and smiling so beautifully, and I can't believe that she even wants to just hang out with me. Make music with me.

Her voice was tender, heavy with love.

"'My Life,'" Tom said quietly. There was a pause.

"Frank Sinatra?" Ramona asked.

"No," Tom said, "Billy Joel."

I opened my eyes. The sun was starting to set.

"You have *got* to be kidding me!" Ramona screamed.

Tom slid off the roof of the car and rolled his eyes. "It's not that weird," he cried as we climbed into the car.

"Yes, yes it is," Ramona said.

Tom turned the car toward my place. Mom was making beef Wellington for dinner and wanted Tom's and Ramona's help eating it, if it turned out right and we don't end up ordering Korean.

Ramona turned around in the front passenger seat to make sure I was listening in the back.

"He uses sound effects. Do you two understand what I'm telling you? Sound effects. Like car engines and work whistles. Wait—is that why you like Billy Joel, Tom? Is it the sound effects?"

"I don't care what you say anymore, this is *my life*!" Tom sang, apparently over his shame. "Go ahead with your own life and leave me—"

All I'm thinking about is Ramona's voice.
I always knew that she loved me,
because you know, friends love
each other. But her voice.
For the first time in years, I wonder
about the impossible.

Tom

Her number is still in my phone

(and all her old

messages).

"Hey," she says. Her voice sounds strange, cautious and new again.

"Hey," I say. "How are you?"

"Good!" There were a few phone calls in the first two weeks after she broke up with me. Those conversations were horrible and entirely my fault. I'm relieved that she even answered. She sounds relieved that I sound civil. "How are you?"

"I'm good," I say. "I was wondering if you maybe wanted to get a cup of coffee sometime? Just a friend thing. I'm seeing someone."

"I would love that, Tom," Sara says. "I really would."

We agree to meet at a coffee place in the Central West End, the neighborhood Sara's family hails from. Tennessee Williams, T. S. Eliot, and William S. Burroughs all grew up here too. I don't think Sara will end up a writer, but she's going to make a mark on the world. I'm certain of that.

I get there first and go ahead and order our coffees. Sara likes heavy-tasting Ethiopian coffee, no sugar, no cream. Sara is always on time, so I know it will still be piping hot when she gets here. I parked right outside the shop, and as she approaches the glass door, I see her notice my car and grin.

Inside, her eyes search the room and find mine. I'm at our table, where we always used to sit.

"Hey," she says, not cautious, just happy to see me. She sits down and reaches behind her head to tighten her ponytail, just as I knew she would. She's still wearing her Saint Joe's uniform even though it's four thirty in the afternoon, because she had student government after classes, and then she stayed even later to deal with some sort of emergency with the upcoming spring bake sale. I already know that before Sara came along, there was only one charity bake sale a year at Saint Joe's. Now there are three a year, and each focuses on a different issue. Under Sara's direction, all the baked goods sold now come with a flyer about the need for mosquito netting and vaccinations, or the continuing need for support in regions where earthquakes and tornadoes happened a year ago.

This is the thing about Sara that makes her so special. She sips her crazy caffeinated coffee and talks excitedly about educating her wealthy classmates about world poverty, and there's no bitterness in her voice, no malice. She's just using all the tools at her disposal to make the world a better place. Right now it's student government, but someday it might be the world's largest nonprofit organization. Humans need people like Sara. We need sincere people who are able to work within the system and get people organized for the greater good. I'm pretty sure that there are not a lot of people out there who can do that.

And I love talking to Sara. She's a great listener, which means she actually listens instead of just waiting for her turn to talk, and she nods and frowns and smiles, and you can tell she actually gives a fuck about what you are saying.

I tell her about my idea at Christmas to do some sort of commentary of American consumer culture, and how I put that project aside after I realized that I was just a sheltered punk kid thumbing my nose at the grown-ups.

"But you shouldn't give it up," Sara says. "The message is still a good one. You got a dose of reality when you saw that picture of the starving baby. Now use it. Speak up for that child."

I tell her all about meeting Ramona and Sam, and all about our band, how I'm making the best music I've ever made because of these guys.

"Sam seems sweet. I don't really know Ramona," Sara says. "She just looks so intimidating. I feel like such a nerd next to her."

"Ramona is a badass," I agree. "But she's nice. Really. And Sam, he is sweet and quiet, but he's more than that. He's an amazing guy." I nod and feel the corners of my mouth turn up as I think about them, my best friends.

"Sam is amazing, huh?" Sara says. Her eyes spark up. She sets her cup down on the table and leans forward expectantly.

"Yeah," I say. "He's definitely my best friend. And Ramona. She's my girlfriend now."

The muscles around Sara's eyes twitch.

"Tom," she says.

"I want to be with her," I say, because it's true. I want to be with Ramona. I've become attached to holding her. I like the way she smells. Kissing her is nice, and I love her.

"Why did you invite me here?" Sara says. "Are you trying to prove something?"

"No! I missed you. I miss being friends with you."

"I've missed you, Tom. And I want to be friends with you. I'm ready to see you that way now. But you've got to come to terms with your sexuality."

"I don't have a sexuality!" I tell her, and I shout it, so I guess I'm telling everyone.

Sara looks around nervously and puts a finger to her lips. "Tom—"

"You were the first person I'd ever met who I wanted to see and talk to every day," I tell her, lowering my voice. "You were the first person who ever seemed to understand and accept me. I wanted to be with you more than I ever wanted to be with anyone before. And I loved holding you. And I even liked kissing you, because I loved you. But because my body isn't interested in doing more, you left me. It made my love less valuable to you.

"I didn't think I would ever feel that way about anybody again. Until I met Ramona. And Sam. I love them. I want to be with them."

"Them?" Sara says.

"Yes," I say.

Sara shakes her head. "Tom, you've really got to get this figured out," she says.

"I know exactly who I am," I say.

"Does Ramona?"

I am silent. I start to drink my coffee, and Sara lets the silence sit. She picks her cup and takes a large gulp.

"I should go soon," she says. "It was nice catching up, Tom."

♡x♡Ramona

Have you ever met someone and you could feel that they were going to be important to you? It's like you never knew it, but you've been waiting your whole life to meet this person, and you recognize him with the same ease that you recognize your reflection.

That happened to me twice.

There isn't a love poem for this.

Sam is playing his video game, and Tom has hooked up his kaosolator so that he can make music with the game's sound effects. Needless to say, this music sounds nothing like the original Foleys, yet this music matches the adventure story in a funny, poignant way.

Sam's quiet laugh. Tom's mischievous chuckle.

Oh, how I love both of them.

I'm stretched out on the couch behind them after an amazing practice where we took our music to another level *again*. My triceps and biceps ache, and when I get home I need to practice Liszt's Transcendental Étude No. 10 again because John says that I should have it perfect by now. Really, I've never been happier because my life has never been more full of music and love, even though, yes, it hurts.

Sam strikes the killing blow with his sword with his game controller, and Tom's music swells dramatically, hilariously. The boys high-five.

I love how they laugh together. I love how Tom is able to get mellow, dreamy Sam excited. I love making music with them in pairs and as a trio. I love listening to them as they make music together. I love how Sam can get hyper Tom to stop and think, just like he can with me. I love it when they tease me together.

I love them. Their friendship is at the center of my mind's maze, and their love is the highest-flying banner on my heart. Loving one does not take love away from the other. There isn't a limit to the amount of love I can feel.

There isn't a limit to how much I can love, and this knowledge makes me want to fly. Lying here on the couch, I feel as if I could lift off and away.

The boys laugh and grin at each other.

This love makes me want to love everyone more. Everyone.

It makes me want to at least stop hating Emmalyn.

"You got this, man!" Tom says. "Now back to Hyrule!" The electronic music seems to cry with encouragement too. Sam squares his shoulders and leans over the controller in determination. My arms relax into the couch; my breathing slows. I watch them together and feel my heart beating steady, steady, steady.

Sam

Earlier today I sat next to Ramona on the piano bench and turned pages for her. Since I can read music it wasn't too hard, but she still had to give me a nod sometimes. It was distracting, seeing how nimble her fingers had to be to take the notes I saw on the page and make them into the notes I was hearing, stretching out her thumbs, third and fourth fingers so far across the keyboard.

Between runs, she'd shake her hands and stretch, stretch her arms over her head, stretch her fingers all the way to the very tips, her whole being focused on her body, tranquil and strong, Ramona.

Her boob sometimes brushed my arm when she did this too.

When she was done practicing, Ramona pushed herself off the bench and flung herself onto the living room floor. The condo's living room is not that big, and the piano takes up a lot of space. She would have been in danger of hurting herself if she wasn't so practiced at doing it. I think she's been flinging herself off that piano bench her whole life.

"Tom wants to teach me yoga," Ramona said. Her tone gave these words more gravity than the statement should have had.

"Oh?" I stayed seated on the piano bench. I had a good view of her there.

"Yeah. He always wants to do physical things with me." Hopefully, I didn't make a face when she said that, but she added quickly, "We do a lot of urban hiking. The River des Peres was fun. We made a wind chime out of the bicycle wheel and glass bottles we found there."

"That's cool."

"We make a lot of art. And listen to music. And we talk a lot. Then he drives me home."

I felt like Ramona was trying to tell me something, or maybe she's trying to tell it to herself, but neither of us was getting the message.

"Sounds fun," I said.

"It is," she said, but something was wrong. She scooted over. I pushed off the piano bench and lay down next to her.

We were quiet. She breathed. I listened. I wanted to be closer to that sound.

Her arm brushed mine as we relaxed into the floor.

My eyes closed.

"It's nice to be still," she whispered. "I'm never still with him."

I was so focused on her that I could hear her hair against the carpet as she turned her head in my direction. I thought that she was looking at me. I kept my eyes closed and waited for her to say something.

She said nothing. She was still with me again.

With me.

Looking at me. Her breath slightly quickened. I couldn't stop the slow smile that creased my face. Ramona sighed, and I thought it's for me. Ramona sighed, and I was sinking into the floor as my soul flew up past the ceiling. Ramona sighed, and I realized that I never knew how she felt about me, because I never had anything to compare it too, because it was always just the two of us, being still together.

Tom

Suddenly it is spring. It is the time of spring when
people say it has sprung. Birds are building a nest
on the roof of my parents' porch, and even crab-
grass is green again.
It's been windy too, the kind of wind that makes me
want to run, to drive long distances.
At school the teachers leave the windows open, and
the rest of the world, the rest of my life,
feels so close and so far away.

We're all lying on the concrete floor of the garage with
the door open for the breeze, and just a few moments ago
Ramona said,

"In four months, we'll be moving into the dorms at
Artibus." And no one said anything. We all just thought our
thoughts.

❧

I'm not going to Artibus College. It's crazy that
I ever thought I might go there, because I'm not
going to go to college anywhere. It's crazy
that I ever thought I would. That I could.
I want to be educated. I want to read books at the
time of my choosing. I want to listen to classical
composers and modern jazz and drive across the
country. I want to make my music and my art, and
give it away as gifts to the people that I meet.
I don't want a career, just to be able to find work
when I need it.
I don't want to buy a house.
I don't know if I'll ever want a family.
I want to figure out my life as it happens to me.
I want to make my own way.
I want to find my own ambitions,
and to strive for what *I* value.
Yes.
Someday my mind may change, but I can't make myself
plan for a future I know I don't want right now. And
making plans doesn't make you safe; it just makes
you feel that the future owes you something.

I squeeze Ramona's hand, and she squeezes mine back. I owe her an explanation for why I did nothing after she placed my hand on her left breast last night. I owe her something. That's what being in a relationship is, and if I can't give this to her, I need to tell her now. Soon.

And I know, that if I want to live the
life of my choosing, it's time
I'm honest about myself.

"I'm not going to Artibus," I tell them.

"What are you talking about?" Ramona cries. "You have to go to college with us!"

♡x Ramona

"I can't," he says. "I'm sorry."

I sit up too quickly. My head spins.

On either side of me, the boys push themselves up.

"We have to go," I tell them. "We *all* have to go."

We have to stay together. We have to

keep the music together.

I can't free fall into adulthood without them.

Without Sam, how will I stay sane?

Without Tom, how will I be brave?

"I'm not going to college. I think I've

known that for a while now."

"Oh no, Tom," I say.

"Ramona?" Sam says. "There's something

I have to tell you too. I'm sorry, but I'm—"

Sam isn't coming to Artibus. Tom

isn't going to college at all.

I'm falling. I'm melting. I'm barely listening.

My security has been shattered, my
safety net pulled loose. My head has filled
with cement; my heart's been set on fire. It's
all too much to handle, far too much to hold.
"Guys," I say, "I don't feel well. Somebody
needs to take me home."
And we go together, just the way
I thought we were supposed to be,
except now I am
alone.

Sam

Ramona missed school after I told her I wasn't going to Artibus or majoring in music at all.

I should have told her that I never applied to Artibus. I could have told her when I filled out the application for Saint Louis University, or even when my acceptance letter came. Any time before would have been better, but when Tom had dropped his bomb, I knew I couldn't hold out any longer.

After school Tom came over and we sat in the silent garage.

"We should have told her sooner," I said to him. He nodded.

"I knew she would be disappointed, but I never thought she would be so devastated. And I thought she would still have you."

"And I thought she would have you. Are you really not going to college at all?"

He shrugged.

"Maybe someday I will. I want to travel and do my own

studying first. But that doesn't mean that I'm going to stop being with you and Ramona."

I felt myself smile.

"I'm not going to let that happen either," I said.

My father lives a life of neat boxes.
He chooses the people in his life by what
expected function
they can provide him.
He loves me, within limitations.
I love Ramona for who she is, for loving music and humans
so fiercely.
She loves Tom for the same reasons I do: for his passion
and his idealism, his hidden vulnerability.
My father would want me to separate Ramona and Tom.
Have me secure Ramona in a Girlfriend box
and lock Tom far away from her in a Just Friends box.
My father has very little love in his life.
My father has never had friends like Ramona and Tom.

The next day, Ramona came to school. She smiled and said, "Hey." She drummed on the picnic table and talked about math class, but it was obvious everything was still wrong. A spark had gone out; her smiles were too slow. Her hope for the future has turned into fear.

I texted Tom. He told me he had a plan.

I'd hoped he would say something like that.

Tom will know what to do for our Ramona.

Tom

There's an empty warehouse near the Mississippi River with high, tall, broken windows that take in all of the afternoon's sun. I scouted out this location weeks ago, but I didn't know what would go here. It was a place to make an avowal; I knew that much.

Now Ramona needs a declaration. She thinks high school will be the end of us, the end of Vandalized by Glitter.

It's time I told her (them) how I feel.

Yesterday, I started making the stencil. Today is the day of execution.

I sent Sam the address, but it takes them an hour to find me through the unused streets and forgotten buildings of the riverboat industry.

"Tom?" Sam calls, standing at the broken door. He holds one hand over his eyes, squinting in the sun. Ramona, pale and quiet, peers around his shoulder. "That you, Tom?"

"Yeah," I say. "Come on in."

They step toward me, and I see their eyes shift from my face to over my shoulder to the crumbling brick wall behind me.

In the brightest blue paint I could find, I painted three intertwined circles on the dirty redbrick wall. Each circle shares a part with the others'; each circle has a part in the center.

Underneath that, I've added, *THINK DIFFERENTLY, LOVE MORE.*

"So the way I see it," I say, "Ramona is the heart. And, Sam, you're our equal sign. I'm the question mark." I point to each of them in turn. I'm nervous. What I'm trying to say is kind of a big deal.

"And the circles. We're all our own person. We're all a part of each other. We are all of us together.

"When I'm with you guys, I see the world in new ways. I'm less cynical. I think connecting with you guys has, like, opened up my heart. I care about other people more, every-body more. What I'm trying to say is—" Suddenly the truth of what I am saying gives me the confidence I need.

"This isn't just a high school thing," I tell them. "I'd been waiting my whole life to meet you guys. You're a part of me now, and no matter where any of us goes, I know I'm gonna know you for forever."

It's like I've let go of the trapeze first, and I don't know if they will want to catch me or not.

They step closer to me.

Ramona takes my hand and then Sam's. I touch Sam on his shoulder. He meets my eyes and nods.

We stand together in the sunlight pouring down upon us.

♡xoRamona

Emmalyn's mother took a long time to die. That's how Ava Schumacher put it to me in the girls' bathroom. I know it's weird that I asked her about it, but it was also kinda weird how eager Ava was to tell me about it. It's just that I needed to know.

My mother took a long time to die too.

Cancer hits the body like ocean waves. It recedes, dies back like autumn, and is reborn in the spring. Like hope, it lingers.

My mother died when I was nine, and I remember her two ways.

I remember her at the piano, playing for me, teaching me, touching me, the keys, my fingers, her fingers. Her voice in my ear as we practiced, low and encouraging, firm, never scolding.

I remember her on the couch, too sick to get up and sit at the piano. I played for her until she would smile. Her smiles were frail, often sleepy. I remember the bones of her face, the rattle of her chest, the whisper of her breaths. I remember the hospital bed we lay in together, the sheet music, and the electronic keyboard.

There is another prominent memory from those years. I went to a hippie charter school that pushed freethinking and health food. My classmates weren't ridiculously rich, but they could all read, and I only sort of could.

I could tell you all the sounds of the letters. That wasn't a problem. I had been fine when it came to learning that. But once the letters were arranged together for words Iw as lo st.

The l ett ers mo ved a nd rea rranged

and

lit tle *d* was ide ntical to l it ttle *b* db db bd db

At first, it was just that I took a little longer to read than my classmates, and because I was still obviously bright, no one was worried. But suddenly (one day, so suddenly, it seemed to me), I was DELAYED in reading. I couldn't finish reading assignments on time, or even at all. The teachers recommended my parents seek a DIAGNOSIS.

"DYSLEXIA?" my mother said. "But she can read music just fine." She had been well enough to come to the appointment. Her floral headscarf was the brightest thing in the office, until she said those words and I felt my face get warm.

It had been easy to fake. When my mother quizzed me on the notes, I knew their names. Looked at individually, I could read the note, hum the tone. But when I sat at the piano and tried to st r ing t he no tes to get her my ey es could not foll ow.

However, when my mother sat down to help me with the piece, all I had to do was watch her hands, and I would know what to do. Before long, I was able to stare straight ahead uncom prehe n ding ly, at the sheet music, and play from memory the song I'd been instructed to learn.

When my mother understood what had been happening, she wasn't angry with me. She was heartbroken. She felt that she had failed me.

"I should have known," she kept saying. Again, she tried to teach me to read music, but every teaching session ended in tears.

I still played for her when she lay on the couch. I played all the songs I knew from memory. But her eyes would stay sad even when she smiled. When I told her that I hadn't meant to lie to her, she hugged me and told me that she knew, that she would always love me and be proud of me.

My parents hired a reading tutor who came twice a week. Her name was Miss Judy. She covered texts with cards so that I could see one

Letter

at a time. Then one

Word

at a time

until I could read lines of text aloud at a slow but reasonable rate.

Mom had to go back into the hospital around then. We didn't know it, but she wasn't coming home. Miss Judy wanted me to read for twenty minutes every day, and suddenly Dad was acting like this was more important than piano.

Twice I had screaming meltdowns because Dad wouldn't let us go to the hospital until I'd done that day's reading.

Mom stopped responding to treatment, but there was an experimental drug doctors wanted to try.

When I told Mom about playing piano, she didn't respond as eagerly as she always had before. She always wanted to know how reading was going. Stressful, upsetting reading—it seemed like that was all anyone cared about anymore.

Finally, Mom and Dad told me that the doctors were

moving her to hospice. Hospice wasn't a new way of fighting cancer. The fight was over; cancer had won.

Mom was still alive, but her life was over. She'd toured Europe as a professional musician; she'd had a husband and child. It wasn't a bad life, but it was over, and it was all she would ever have.

I was the only child my mother ever had, and as she smiled at me from her pink-sheeted hospice bed, I finally realized that unless I learned to read music, my promise as a pianist had come to an end. I could love music, I could feel as if I lived for music, but I would never be a musician if I could only play what I'd learned from watching my mother.

Every day after school, I did my twenty minutes of reading practice, and then Dad and I went to see Mom. She had a keyboard there in her room, always set to grand piano, and with it, she helped me practice reading sheet music for hours, until we were both too tired to continue.

Until Mom didn't continue to be anymore.

I passed third grade with an average score in reading.

And I was playing through Mom's old sheet music so fast that Dad realized that it would be worthwhile to replace Miss Judy with a piano instructor.

Anyway.

That's the story of how my mother died and how I became a musician.

I don't know how Emmalyn's mother died, but I know that it's the story of how Emmalyn became the person that she is, and it's the story of every person that she will ever be.

And because I am someone with a story, someone who is more than just who I am in my worst moments, I know that I can't judge Emmalyn because I don't really know her. I only know some of her actions these past few years.

So even if I never hug her, maybe it would be worth it to make peace with her before we never see each other again. We're about to start our adult lives. Maybe she'd like to start it with a clean slate too.

Sam

"Hey," I said. We'd just gotten off the highway where we'd rolled the windows down and dragged our hands through the air and sunshine. We'd had a half day of school, and the afternoon was ours.

"Hey," she said, grinning at me, suspecting nothing. I looked away again and rolled all the windows back up so that she'd hear me clearly.

"I love you," I said. I only had time to glance over at her surprised face. I'd decided to do this while driving in my car because driving soothes me, and that way she couldn't leave until I'd finished saying what I had to say. "I'm sorry if that's a problem. And I want us to be friends no matter what. But anyway, I love you, and maybe I'm crazy, but I think there's a chance that you love me too. So if you do, I think we should be together."

"Sam," she asked, "are you serious?"

"Yeah," I said. I nodded to reinforce the point. We'd come to a red light, and I slowed the car to a stop.

"I love you too," she said. I'd never heard Ramona's voice so quiet.

"Really?" I turned to face her so quickly that my neck popped. When I looked at her, she was laughing at me, and there were tears in her eyes.

"Oh, Sam," she said. I took one hand off the steering wheel and laid it over hers. Her lips parted. Behind us a car horn honked, and we both jumped. I had to turn away from her and look at the road.

"But, Sam, I love Tom too. I know that it isn't supposed to be possible to sincerely love two people at once, but it's true. I swear I do."

"I know!" I said. And I do know it. Ramona is full of love. Again, I only had a chance to glance at her surprised face, but my speech was prepared and I was ready to launch into it. "And I love Tom too. I don't have sexual feelings for him, but I love him. He's massively important to me. He's somebody I want to see and talk to every day, just like you.

"I love you, and he loves you, and I know he loves me too, and I think that we can all work this out. I mean, we'll have to talk to Tom about this obviously, but if everybody loves everybody, why should that be a problem? Why can't we all just be together?"

I'd timed it perfectly, and we'd just pulled into the parking space outside the condo. I took the keys out of the ignition and finally turned in my seat toward her. The mix of emotions on her face was too much for me to gain any information.

She paused, tears still in her eyes, then said, "You're serious about this, aren't you?"

I nodded.

"Do you remember last week, when we were all lying on the garage floor together?" I asked. "You were holding Tom's hand and I was on your other side, and I thought that if I could just hold your hand too, I would be happy. It wouldn't bother me that you were holding Tom's hand too, because I love Tom too. So, yeah, if Tom's okay with it, I'm serious about this.

"Ramona, you are extraordinary. You're smart and hilarious and full of life. I don't want to own you. I just want to be near you and to love you."

When I used the L word again, I laid my hand over hers once more and waited.

"Oh, Sam, I don't know. I just don't know," she said. She started crying for real then, and I got to hold her while she cried on my shoulder and explained to me everything she did not know.

Tom

"TOM!"

I slam my locker shut and turn around.

"Ally?" I say.

"Did you forget that today was the last day to sign up for the senior showcase?"

"I did not."

"So you're headed to Ms. Beasley's before lunch?"

"I am not."

"TOM!"

"Ally," I say, "I would thank you for your concern, but you don't want me to perform in the showcase for my sake. This is about your legacy, not mine." I'm about to turn away from her toward the cafeteria when her shrill cry stops me again.

"TOM! That is true for most of the people I have been harassing the past few weeks. But in your case, I am sincere."

I don't answer her, and this seems to be all of the encouragement she needs.

"You have kept yourself apart from everybody, always. It's probably been for the best, because you don't fit in with most people and you know that."

Again, I don't answer her, and she continues.

"Tom, I've always admired you. Seriously. You're different. Everybody knows it. And to most people that's intimidating, but I've had two great dads telling me I'm amazing my whole life, so I'm down with it. Anyway, because most people are intimidated by you, most people haven't really given you a chance. Now *is* your chance."

"Bye, Ally," I say. I start to turn, but she grabs my arm.

"TOM! This is about your legacy. You're not coming back. You aren't gonna be at the reunions. You know it; I know it. This is your only chance to say to everybody, 'This is who I am!' Who cares what they think?"

"I don't."

"Exactly."

"Ally..."

"Finish high school by thumbing your nose at everybody who discounted you. Declare your identity as a weirdo and say sayonara. Just because you're giving people something to look back on doesn't mean that you're the one looking back."

"Ally…"

"Tom?"

♡✗Ramona

There's a park right across the street from the condo. That's where I take Tom to have our conversation.

"I used to play here when I was little," I tell him.

"Yeah?" he says. He knows I'm acting strange, and his face shows his worry. I keep talking.

"Suburban kids have backyards, and *maybe* they have a swing set," I say. "But I had a whole playground and a lake with ducks." I sit down on the bench facing the jungle gym. Tom slumps down next to me, his head hanging. He looks exactly like he did the day we met him, miserable and alone.

"Tom?" I say.

"Yeah?"

"I love you." We've never said that to each other before, not explicitly. He'd been staring at his knees. Now he looks up and meets my eyes.

"I love you too," he says, but he says it like he's waiting for a trap to spring.

"But you don't want me, do you?" I say. I keep my gaze steady and kind. Again, he slumps in his seat and stares at the ground.

"I should have told you," he says, "but when I told Sara, she abandoned me. I don't want to lose you, Ramona."

"I'm not going to abandon you, Tom," I say. "That's not what love is."

He takes a deep, shuddering breath, and my heart breaks for him.

"It's not that I don't want you, Ramona. It's that I don't want anybody. I never have. I don't think I ever will. Nothing happened to me. The doctor said there's nothing wrong with my body. Please believe me. I know that I love you, and I really do think that I am in love with you. But sex isn't something I can give you. It's just not in me."

I take a moment to think about this.

This seems like something that could happen in the course of nature.

He's the same Tom; I just didn't know this about him before.

I still want to be with him. I'm just going to have to adjust how I see him, what I expect from him.

"Okay."

"What?"

I shrug. "I mean, sex isn't something *I* wanna live

without, and that's related to the other thing we gotta talk about, but okay."

He throws his arms around me with such force that I'm knocked backward, and we nearly fall off the bench. I can't help it; I laugh.

And Tom says, "You don't think I'm lying or in denial or a freak?"

And I can't help but laugh again.

"No, I think you're just Tom," I say. He squeezes me tight and I return the hug, relishing how nice to is to be held by someone who loves you. "I have to tell you something now," I finally say.

"Yeah?" He pulls back.

"Sam's in love with me."

His face falls. He sighs.

"I know," he says.

"You do?"

"I've known that for a long time. When did you find out?"

"Today. Tom," I say, and now I'm the one taking a deep breath. "I'm in love with him too."

"Oh. You are?" His head is cocked to the side. He's surprised. He isn't angry. He looks worried, but he continues to hold my hand.

"Sam says that he doesn't want to break us up," I say quickly. "He said that he just wants to be with me too and stay friends with you."

"Well, that's perfect then," Tom says.

"What?" I say. Apparently it's my turn.

"That's perfect. We can all just be together then."

"You don't think it's a weird idea?"

"It is a weird idea. That doesn't mean it's a bad idea."

I laugh and bump my head against his shoulder one last time, at least for a while.

"I'm gonna have to take some time to adjust how I see you," I tell him. "We should probably not be affectionate with each other for a little while. I need to be able to put our physical relationship in context."

Tom squeezes my hand. Then he lets it go.

"I do really love holding your hand, holding you," he says. "And I like kissing you." We talk about what he likes and what he feels less enthusiastic about. He asks me about my conversation with Sam. Then he asks me where Sam is.

"At home I guess," I say. "I told him I needed to talk to you."

"Could we go see him?" Tom asks. "We need to have a band meeting. There's a favor I need to ask you guys. About the senior showcase at my school."

Sam

"You signed us up to participate in a school activity?" I asked. We were all sitting on the floor of the garage in a circle. Ramona had her hand in mine, which added to the dreamlike quality of the conversation. We were all sitting together, and everything was different, and everything was the same. "You want Vandalized by Glitter to perform at your school's 'senior showcase'?"

"Yes," Tom said. "It's not like me to leave without making a mark. I want to show our music to my classmates."

"I suppose Vandalized by Glitter needs to have a practice show," Ramona said. She wasn't holding hands with Tom right then, but someday, she's gonna be holding his hand too, and I won't mind that 'cause she'll still be holding mine.

"Yeah, I mean, we don't need to make a big deal out of this or anything," Tom said. I laughed, given the context of our situation.

"So!" Ramona jumped up, still holding my hand, dragging my arm up with her. How I love her. "We need to finish mixing the album. That way we can have it up for download on the website, in case a few of your classmates do actually like our music. And then we need to pick—how long did you say our set could be? Fifteen minutes? So we need to pick probably two of our songs and practice them a ton, so that maybe a few of your classmates actually like our music!"

Tom had already stood up. I pushed myself up with one hand, still reluctant to let go of Ramona. (I hadn't kissed her yet, but I realized that I would soon. That I would drive her home that night—)

"All right, we better get to work," I said. "It's a school night, and I can't be up that late."

Tom

"There's something I want to talk to you guys about," I say to Mom and Dad. It's dinnertime. I'm supposed to be talking to my parents about my life, sharing my feelings and such. My parents and I have spent most of my adolescent years in a battle over my reluctance to tell them anything about myself. I expect them to be overjoyed at my words. I thought that this conversation would start with their pleasure at my involving them in my life.

Instead they look startled. And suspicious. There's nothing for me to do but plow ahead.

"This is one of those things where I'm gonna ask that you don't say anything until I finish. Okay?" This doesn't improve their demeanor, but again, all I can do is continue. "I don't want to go to Artibus. I know that it was a great place for Jack. But I don't think it's right for me. I know that you guys just want what's best for me, so I want to tell you what I think that is.

"Teddy says that he wants to hire me for real at Grift Craft, on the books and everything. I like working there. I'm good at talking to people about art supplies. Teddy is planning on opening this other business with a friend of his. He'll be getting pretty busy this summer, and he says he'll bump me up to full time by autumn.

"I don't want a career in retail, but I'd like to work there for a few years. I'll pay rent if you want. I'm also going to still be reading books, trying to work my way through the classics and the important works of nonfiction, and I'll be studying music. I'll still be educating myself, I swear.

"I'm gonna live by a budget and save as much money as I can. When I feel like I have enough money in the bank, I want to buy a car—the most environmentally friendly one that I'd still be able to live out of sometimes—and I'd like to travel the continent, see as much as I can. I can live very cheaply, and stay at hostels and communes—Let me finish, Mom—even stay in some places doing temporary work. Manual labor will be fine.

"I could stretch my money and be able to travel for a few years, really get to see the world. And I'll still be reading and watching documentaries. What I'm trying to say, guys, is that I want to pursue my own path of education. I'm not sure where I'm going to end up ultimately, but most college students don't know either—and the ones who are certain about what they're going to do might be wrong anyway.

"This is really what I want, guys. I don't want to pursue making as much money as possible. I want to pursue seeing and experiencing as much as possible."

My parents stare at me from across the table.

"You. Are planning. On being. Homeless," my mother says.

It doesn't really get better from there.

At one point I shout at my father, "They don't use heroin in communes, Dad!"

Mom screeches back, "You can't possibly know that, Tommy!"

It only ends hours later by us all admitting that we're getting nowhere. The only thing to do is to not talk about it for at least a week and then try to sit down and calmly discuss this at a later time.

I can't believe I'd actually thought this conversation might go okay.

♡ xo Ramona

Today, we are flyering St. Louis. This is a message for every neighborhood, so it's gonna take all day.

Tom made the flyer. It's his art project, obviously. It's simple, thin white paper with cheap black ink; he emphasized the thrift. Across the top it says:

LOST CHILD

Under that, there's a picture of a baby. I hope it survived. Then,

HAVE YOU EVER
THOUGHT ABOUT
WORLD HUNGER?

and the URL for a website he made that has statistics about regions with chronic undernourishment and directs visitors to charities that provide food and to nonprofits that provide paths to sustainability.

It's not much, but like Tom said, maybe it will get a few people interested, maybe a couple of donations will be made. It's something.

I'm carrying the flyers. Sam has the staple gun for telephone poles, and Tom has the clear packaging tape for light posts. We've posted twenty-three flyers so far. Twenty-seven to go.

Sam keeps looking over at me with this soft, stunned look on his face. It like he's suddenly remembering that we're together. I didn't know that I was capable of being this happy. I wish everyone could feel this way. I wish everyone could be as loved as me.

"Here," Tom says. "Right next to this Lost Dog poster. We want it to almost blend in, so that when people see it, they're startled. We want people to react emotionally to the image before their brain can tell them that it's not their problem."

Tom is the same as ever but perhaps more at ease, more like the earlier days of our friendship. It does make me sad that I won't have those things I'd imagined having with him, but I fell in love with him because he was such a fey character, and I can't fault him for it now. I'll adjust to this, and when he touches me, my body will understand his attentions. He'll still hold me and kiss me and call me his "kiddo." As soon as I say I'm ready.

If he'd demanded monogamy of me,

I couldn't have stayed though.

Though if you'd asked me before,

I would have demanded monogamy.

But now here we are.

I have Sam, my Sam, who was always my Sam.

And Tom. I have Tom.

Strange, beautiful Tom.

We're hanging flyers together;

the guys look at each other and laugh.

We're hanging flyers because we have hope.

We have hope for the world's future, hope for our own.

What's wrong with Hope? What's wrong with Love?

Sam

My girlfriend is drumming.

My girlfriend? She's a great drummer. The greatest drummer, really. She drums like a demon, like a maniac on time. She bangs like a typhoon. She taps like a queen.

I'm damn proud of her, proud to be her boyfriend. Yup, I'm her boyfriend. That's a fact. I've kissed her and smelled her behind her ear. Her. Ramona. My girlfriend.

I strum my sitar and watch her keep our pace. Tom's running effects on the board. Out of the kaosolator comes the sound of a dance-party elven forest gong.

We're playing at Tom's senior showcase in two weeks. This will be Vandalized by Glitter's first public performance, our last one as high school students. A few venues in St. Louis allow musicians under twenty-one to perform. Tom's gonna talk to Teddy about making local booking connections. By July everyone will be eighteen, and we can get at least one show in before Ramona moves into the dorms at

Artibus. After that, she'll come back to St. Louis some week-ends for shows, and she'll find a place near her school where we can perform, for when we visit her there.

Tom says he's leaving in a few years' time. His parents have realized that they can't legally force him into school, and it's not like they can kick him out to punish him for planning to be homeless. Negotiations are in process.

His plans are something I would never choose, but I'm happy for him, that he knows what he wants. I look forward to reading his emails with Ramona. We'll phone, chat online, and visit.

My girlfriend stops drumming. She wipes her sweaty brow.

I love watching her drum. She's a talented musician, and her boobs do amazing things while she's playing.

"We're amazing," she says. "We've gotta run through it again."

Tom

Back at the kitchen table.

This is where my parents sat and talked with my brother Matt after he got his then-girlfriend, now-wife pregnant for the unplanned first time. Now we spend Christmases at their house with their four kids. A picture from the hasty wedding hangs on display. Everybody is happy, and nobody remembers that the existence of my nephew Cody started out in such contention. I don't remember it either. I was only two at the time, but I've heard the stories, and everybody knows this is where we go for Big Talks.

This is also where my favorite brother, Steven, told my parents he was gay. That conversation was just awkward. I hope that in the future, kids can just bring whomever they're dating home without any sort of announcement. There are already enough awkward puberty conversations with parents. Adding a "So, I only like people with these kinda genitals" conversation is just cruel and unusual.

My other brother, Jack, sat with my parents here when he told them he wanted to go to Artibus College and study art. My parents had always stressed that pursuit of a practical career was the only choice they would support. Jack convinced them that he would only be happy working in the arts. He went to Artibus. He's a graphic designer now, and he seems pretty happy.

This is what my parents were hoping for with me. I told them I wanted to study art and music. They said, "Fine. You can go to Artibus like your brother." They sent me to the audition. They reminded me to mail the application. They envisioned me in some sort of job like Jack's.

They thought that they had avoided this conversation. This table.

"You don't know what you're going to want in the future," Mom keeps saying.

"No one does," I say. "And if I want to go to college in the future, then I will."

"I don't understand why you can't just go to Artibus," my mother says later.

"Do you understand why I can't just go into the military? Or just go to seminary?" I ask. "It's not right for me."

"Everyone has to work, Tom," my dad says.

"I going to work," I tell them again. "I'm going to be working hard. And educating myself. And living frugally. Listen to my plan again."

They critique the plan. I make adjustments.

It gets late. We're still at the table.

In the end, it's gridlock. I agree to take one community college course at a time while I'm working at Grift Craft. We agree on rent. They tell me that if I ever want to go to school full-time and work part-time, the rent would be suspended. I thank them and manage not to declare that the offer is unnecessary. I promise them that when I'm on my travels, I'll call, email, maintain a bank account, and keep up my hygiene. My mother presses her lips.

I know they're hoping that my priorities will change after

I meet a nice girl. Or boy. But I won't. I've already met them, and we'll stay in touch when I travel.

I know that my next two years will be full of research on vehicles, hostels, communes, and couch surfing.

It's late. We push in our chairs. Mom hugs me, and Dad sighs and claps me on the back. They love me, even if they don't understand me, and the conversation has ended well enough for all of us.

♡xoRamona

"I really cannot emphasize enough how beautifully you played tonight," my father says to me. "Every day I think, 'I wish her mother could see her,' but tonight—"

We're soaring toward the Arch on the highway. The summer solstice is six weeks away; the sun is only just setting, the lights only just starting to glow. Night is beginning. My father clears his throat.

"Tonight it felt like your mother was here," he says. Tonight was the Saint Joseph Symphonic Exhibition. I'm actually wearing makeup—and the pearls my mother wore when she was touring Europe. In my lap I have three sets of roses.

Red ones from Sam. Yellow from Tom.

Orange from both of them.

I took an orange one and found

Emmalyn in the lobby.

I handed the rose to her.

I said, "I was always just trying to be myself.

I'm sorry we didn't get along."

She said, "Sorry I talked about you out loud like that.

You're right. That was lame."

And now we won't have to hate each other at graduation.

"Thank you, Daddy," I say. He's never told me before that every day he wished Mom could see me. He doesn't mention Mom much—hardly ever, really—but I played Bach tonight, and he was her favorite.

"I'm proud of you. You've worked hard."

"Music is the second most important thing," I say. That was something my mother would always say. We've stopped saying it out loud, but I think it all the time.

The most important thing is love.

"That's true," Dad says, his voice quiet again. After a pause, he adds, "Though for me, it's novels. Novels are the second most important thing."

"Oh. Right," I say. I don't know why I'm surprised. Dad's not a musician, and he isn't one of those high school teachers who just couldn't do what they want to do. He's really dedicated to teaching teenagers to appreciate Jane Austen. "That's really specific. Not books or literature. Novels."

"I care about all books. I have tenderness for all literature. But novels are at the heart of my work. They are the
reason I chose this career."

This is more like normal Dad. Rhapsodizing about nov-
elists is far more common than talking about the weather.

"For me, it's just music," I say, feeling as if I am taking
a bold step. "Not piano specifically. The music I make with
Vandalized by Glitter is really important to me too."

"Yes, but remember that there isn't a career for you in
that." He turns the wheel and we glide off the highway toward
our destination. "You've played piano since you were four.
You've been groomed for this. I've kept up all your mother's
connections. Music is a competitive field, and you've got an
advantage in piano."

"I'm going to pursue an emphasis in percussion from
Artibus's conservatory," I say. "I'll still be studying under
their piano master, but I'll also meet with masters of xylophone and marimba and make compositions with claves
and congas—"

"I—" He shakes his head, still looking at the road. We're
almost home. "I don't think this is a good idea, Moany. You
need to focus on the instrument you could have a career
with, making an impression on the masters who could help

you. An emphasis in percussion sounds fun, but it's not practical for you."

"Dad, I really—I'm going to do this. I know it ups the risk factor of this career path, but it's my calling. Mom was called for the piano. I've got something different going on. I love piano, and I love drums."

(I love Sam and I love Tom.)

Dad drives. We arrive home. He doesn't turn off the engine.

"It's scary for every parent when their child leaves the nest. All I want is to feel like you're safe. But I don't think I'll ever feel that way. We used to wake up in the middle of the night terrified that something had happened to you, but there you were, asleep in your bed, safe and sound. If I have trouble believing that you're okay asleep in your own bed—"

He clears his throat again.

"I'm gonna be okay no matter what, Daddy," I say. "I have love in my life. And music. I'll find my way."

"Your mother was headstrong too," he says, and he is finally crying a little bit. I let myself cry too, so that he doesn't feel alone. Plus, he has to comfort me then, and he forgets to be embarrassed about crying in front of his daughter, which should totally be an okay thing, but men are weird.

Anyway.

Love is the most important thing, even when you're both feeling kinda silly, crying in a car with the engine still running.

Sam

"And Ramona is going to start being affectionate with Tom again after a few weeks?" my mother asked. She was working on a Baked Alaska tonight. This gourmet dessert phase is actually kinda sticking around, the way yoga kinda did. Mom's also starting to talk a lot more about the environment. There's a protest she might attend this weekend.

"Yeah," I said. "I don't mind. She'll still be my girlfriend. I'm just telling you so that if you see something, you won't think Ramona is cheating on me."

"This is a very…mature arrangement. Are you sure about this, Sam?"

"Definitely," I said. "I love her. My love doesn't come with strings attached. Tom's a part of her life. He's part of my life. I don't want to mess with what they have. I just want to be Ramona's boyfriend."

Mom sighed.

"I've heard of stranger arrangements," she said. "I guess we'll just have to wait and see how this turns out for you."

"Thanks for being open-minded," I said. "I'm not even going to mention Ramona and Tom to Dad."

She sighed again.

"Your father does tend to see conventionality as a moral obligation."

"Yeah," I said. "Remember how he acted around me after I shaved my legs for swim team in eighth grade?"

Mom laughed at the memory, then frowned. "In his own way, your father loves you very—"

"It's okay, Mom. I know," I said. I shrugged and smiled for her. "I do know that he loves me in his own way. And I think I've figured it out. Dad didn't want children, did he? He just felt like he was supposed to have them."

Mom's frown deepened. It looked as if she was furious with the meringue.

"He told me that he wanted two children. One boy and one girl, as if we could control that. He told me this on our third date. I thought that he was moving our relationship so fast because he was so enamored with me. I understood later that it was simply that he'd met me when he'd decided it was time to get married. He was so much older, and I was swept off my feet.

"I mean it when I say he loves you. He cried when you were born, and that was the only time I ever saw him cry. But he didn't know what to do with you. He didn't understand babies and he didn't want to learn—and he was shocked by how much you intruded on his adult life.

"I think that if he'd listened to his intuition, he would have realized that he didn't actually want to be a father. But you're right. To him it was questionable to not have a child. It's what a person is supposed to do."

The meringue layer was finished. The cake glowed white and pristine. It was supposed to go back into the freezer at that point.

"I'm sorry," Mom said.

I shrugged again. "You've been a great mother, so I'm good." She laughed and ruffled my hair, something she used to do when I was a kid. I ducked away. "Mom! I'm eighteen!"

She sighed for a third time, but this time it's a happy sigh.

"And that means you're all grown up?"

"Obviously."

"Growing up isn't summiting a mountain, you know. There's no end point."

"Sure there is. Maybe you could argue that I'm not an adult because I couldn't afford to live on my own. But I'll get there."

"Yes. But you'll never stop growing. At least, I hope you never do. The people who stop growing are cruel to strangers on the Internet. They're the people who cut you off in traffic and then honk at you." She was cleaning up the kitchen mess now, almost talking to herself.

"They're mean because they're unhappy, and they're unhappy because they're stuck. They're stuck because they're refusing to open their minds, to consider changing the way they live their lives.

"You gotta keep growing and changing, Sammy," Mom said. "You have to listen to new ideas. You have to read up on the other side of the argument. Pain is a part of growing, and you have to learn to forgive yourself as your values change. But if you keep growing, then every year you'll find that you're more comfortable with yourself, with the life you've built, and that makes it easier to be a kinder person to others."

She reached over and ruffled my hair before I could stop her.

"And I'm never going to stop being your mother, no matter how old you are."

"Okay. Wisdom dispensed, Mom. I'm going to my room. Call me when we get to eat the cake." She rolled her eyes and let me head upstairs, and I felt lucky and loved.

Tom

My school doesn't have much of a green room. It's really more of a storage space that's connected to the stage. Most of the stuff that they store back here is related to theater. Most of the stuff. Right now, we three are sitting crammed next to a pair of discarded punching bags from the gym. Ramona has her snare drum in her lap and her tom sitting between me (Tom) and herself. She's still keeping a bit of space from me for now, and I get that. She's holding hands with Sam, but she's smiling a lot at me.

"And then I'll probably go to grad school," Sam is explaining. "I want to go to a school that will allow me to focus on sustainable chemistry, green chemistry that creates products without environmental impact.

"This is something I've thought about for a long time. I'm really good at chemistry, and I want to make the world a better place. But music will always be a massive part of my life. A part of my life's work that I want to look back at on my deathbed. It's just not the only work that I feel called to do."

I nod. Ramona squeezes his hand. This conversation is overdue, but I think he was hesitating because of all the times Ramona and I talked badly about people who wanted to pursue a normal career. I'm not going to make that mistake again. We're all just trying to find our way, and you know, it takes all kinds of people to make a world.

People like Sara.

I'm going to send Sara an email with some links to sites about other people like me. I'm going to tell her about how Ramona and Sam and I are making a go of it. I'm going to tell her that I want us to be friends, that it's up to her whether she can accept me or not.

And hopefully she and I will be friends again soon.

If not, then,

oh well.

Ally has appeared next to us, her clipboard in hand.

"Okay, okay, okay, okay," she says. "Do you have all of your equipment ready? Your setup has to be fast. We're on a tight schedule!"

"Ally," I say, standing up. "Have you met my girlfriend, Ramona, and her boyfriend, Sam, who's also my best friend?" I gesture to them. Ramona waves.

"Hi there." Ally says. "Yes, Tom, you're very weird. Now

focus. You're about to go onstage." She reiterates the importance of a quick sound check and hustles us to the wings of
the stage. Some boys are finishing up Monty Python's coconuts
skit, and King Arthur comes galloping (sort of) toward us.

"Wait for the applause to finish…" Ally tells us. "Okay,
go. Quick sound check!"

The lights are too bright for me to see much past the stage,
but I know my parents are out there, and Ramona's dad and
Sam's mom. We're going to be showing our music to the
world tonight. Sure, we've posted it to the Internet, but the
Internet is practically anonymous. This is our first live performance, and live performance will always be one of the
most important aspects of music.

We set up quickly, like Ally said we needed too. I mic us
all and run it all to the AV teacher's soundboard. We test our
instruments. We look at each other.

I look at beautiful, crazy Ramona, her spiky hair sticking out of her head every which way. She looks at Sam,
solid, tranquil Sam, smiling at her and then looking toward
me. I nod at him, at her, and we turn to face the audience.

"This is Vandalized by Glitter," I say. "Ramona Andrews on drums, Sam Peterson on guitar, and I'm Tom 'the Chaos Maker' Cogsworthy." Sam strikes the opening chord and it floats out over the crowd. Ramona taps one drumstick to the rim of the tom, the other dead in the center. Time speeds up; something is coming. Sam floats us away on the melody. We just can't keep our feet on the ground; we just have to fly. I start in on the kaosolator, playing a preset countermelody that I'm improvising effects on. The something has come. It's trying to drag us down.

We do battle with the forces pulling at us.

Vandalized by Glitter is Victorious Glorious.

Which is why that's the title of that song.

I silence the kaosolator; next to me,

Ramona's drumming slows to a stop.

Sam hits the last note, and the song winds down.

Silence.

One person starts to enthusiastically

clap just as someone else shouts,

"What the hell was that?"

If he says anything else, it's drowned out by polite applause.

Vandalized by Glitter is already getting set up for the next song. Ramona needs the snare drum now; Sam switches to his beloved acoustic guitar.

I turn to face the crowd.

"Hey," I say. "Some of you may not like our music, but

we've got one more song to play for you, and

this song is not for you.

We aren't playing it for you.

We're playing it for ourselves

and anybody out there who might like it.

So.

Just be cool. Okay, guys?"

I look over at Ramona and Sam. Sam gives me a

thumbs-up. Ramona winks.

"This song is for us," I say,

and we play our song.

Acknowledgments

This book would not have been conceived of without the help of Leah Hultenschmidt. Thank you, Leah, for believing in me when I couldn't believe in myself.

This book was bravely taken on by Annette Pollert-Morgan. Thank you, Annette, for all of your support.

Ali McDonald rescued my first novel from her slush pile and now she sends me encouraging emails and treats me like a rockstar. Ali, you are vital to my creative life.

My husband and our friends let me hang out and pretend to be a part of their band for two years. Those guys provided a lot of the inspiration for this novel, and you can check out their music at theicebergsband.com.

I'd like to thank all of the bands and musicians that are referenced in this book, just in case they ever stumble across this book or are watching us all from beyond the grave. Thanks for the music.

Most of all, I'd like to thank all of you for reading this book. You rock.

About the Author

Laura Nowlin is also the author of *If He Had Been with Me* and many other future novels that she just hasn't written yet, okay? You can contact her on Twitter, Tumblr, Goodreads, or Facebook if you should so desire.